Otherwise Engaged

A
SUN VALLEY
LOVE ON VACATION
STORY

KELLIE COATES GILBERT

Otherwise Engaged
Copyright © 2018 Kellie Coates Gilbert

ISBN Paperback: 9780960067725

CHAPTER ONE

Lindsay Griffin had never been so nervous about a party in all her life.

She stepped from the town car and placed her plum-colored Christian Louboutin pumps onto the wet portico driveway, taking special care not to let the de-icing pellets ruin the heels.

"Lindsay Kaye, why didn't you wear boots like I recommended? This is a ski resort, for goodness sakes." Her mother handed off her carry-on to the bellman. Behind, a porter struggled to push a cart filled with their luggage.

Lindsay sighed. "The stores in Atlanta don't carry snow boots, Mama."

Her mother gave her the look, the one she always got when her mom thought she was being insolent. "I'm sure a girl of your age has heard of Amazon. And be careful. You don't want anything splashed on those pants. They cost me a fortune."

"Julia! Lindsay! You finally made it!"

Sheryl DeLuca, her future mother-in-law, scurried through the open doors with arms outstretched wearing a pair of stylish leggings, a tunic-length sweater in shades of teal and a pair of matching Uggs. Tyler's mother air-kissed Julia's cheeks, then turned and hugged Lindsay. "You two are going to love Sun Valley. And this lodge— such a beautiful place. They remodeled recently, upgrading all the amenities." She leaned to Lindsay. "I've booked us girls in the spa on Saturday morning. A great way to kill time before the big party."

Sheryl looked over her shoulder at the luggage trolley. "Is that all the bags you brought?"

Her mother tipped the doorman. "We had the rest of our things shipped ahead."

Tyler's mom placed her arms around their waists and swept them inside. "Like I noted, the lodge recently underwent a renovation to modernize. Didn't the owners do a marvelous job preserving the rich history?"

Sheryl was right. The Sun Valley Lodge was really great. When her mama mentioned the establishment had been built in 1936, she'd immediately imagined old and rustic. Not this.

Plush carpets, pretty draperies on massive windows overlooking a real ice skating rink. Enormous vases of flowers displayed on gorgeous wood tables. Overhead, massive chandeliers hung from a vaulted ceiling and deep rich wood walls flanked a massive fireplace made of rock.

"Did you notice the pool area?" Sheryl motioned for her to follow. She stopped at the windows and pointed. Outside, steam rose from a glass enclosed circular pool bordered by pines heavily laden with snow.

"The pool is outdoors?"

"Oh, yes," Sheryl said, grinning. "The pool is a hallmark of this lodge and is open year 'round."

The entire place looked like something out of one of her mother's Architectural Digest magazines. Everything one might expect from a venue chosen by the DeLucas for her upcoming engagement party.

Her mother joined them. "Oh, just look at that." She clasped her hands with excitement. "An ice skating rink and everything!"

Sheryl grinned back at her. "If you'd like, we can have a private brunch ringside. All it would take is a quick call to Karyn Macadam, the hospitality director. She's been very responsive to all our requests."

Her mother's eyes lit up. "Oh, that would be lovely. A lady on our flight told us the brunches here at the lodge are spectacular."

Sheryl nodded. "I wholeheartedly agree. Normally, they only serve brunch on Sundays, but I know Karyn would make it happen if we ask."

Lindsay stifled a groan. The last thing she wanted was for this engagement party to turn into a spectacle. She'd argued the point on multiple occasions, her mother's pat response always being the same. "Oh, baby. You'll soon be Mrs. Tyler DeLuca. This party needs to reflect that fact."

"I'm not marrying Tyler for his money, Mama."

"Of course you're not, Lindsay Kaye. Your fiancé is brilliant, handsome, connected—a man

4

who has a bright future ahead of him. But it doesn't hurt that he's Charles DeLuca's son."

As if on cue, Tyler and his father appeared in the lobby. Both were dressed in pressed chinos and ski sweaters. Tyler's hair was dark brown while his father's gray, but both men wore their hair clipped short and carefully groomed.

"Hey, babe." Her fiancé leaned and gave her a kiss on the cheek.

"So, you made it." Tyler's dad pulled her into a light embrace, then turned to her mother. "I hope your trip was nice, Julia."

"We had an unexpected layover in Salt Lake, mechanical trouble or something," her mother reported. "But other than that, uneventful. I loved the little airport we flew into."

Charles nodded. "Yes, Friedman is charming."

"And the people at the counter are so friendly," her mom gushed. "Well, everyone here in the Ketchum Sun Valley area seems to be engaging."

Tyler's mother picked a bit of lint from her son's sweater. "We almost built in Vail, but after Charles saw an article in Conde Nast touting the mountains of Idaho, we visited and quickly fell in love with this area."

Lindsay placed her hand on Tyler's arm. "Love the new look. Kind of *"upscale ski bum,"* she teased.

She hadn't seen Tyler in over three weeks. He'd been tied up in a business negotiation in New York while she'd spent the holidays in Atlanta, giving in to her mother's insistence that it might be the last Christmas they had, just the two of them.

"After you get settled, why don't you join me for lunch? Alone." He winked pointedly for their parents' benefit.

His mother looked beside herself with happiness. "Isn't that cute? You two make such a darling couple." And to Julia, "These kids are so adorable."

His dad placed his arm around his wife's shoulder. "A few party guests will be arriving later this afternoon, with most arriving tomorrow. Beyond friends and family, many of the people joining us this weekend are business associates. Julia and I will be hosting a little cocktail party at our condo tomorrow night."

Tyler's mother waved off her husband's comments. "Yes, but we're keeping business to a minimum this weekend, aren't we dear?"

Charles gave a throaty laugh. "Of course, dear."

"Everything sounds wonderful, doesn't it Lindsay?" Her mama turned. "And on that note sweetheart, we'd best head to our room and freshen up."

"*Our* room?" Tyler glanced between Lindsay and her mother. "I thought you were in—"

With a half laugh, her mother shook her head. "Goodness, the Hemingway suite is plenty big enough for both of us. Besides, I thought Lindsay might enjoy the history. Hemingway wrote a portion of *For Whom the Bell Tolls* in that room. Isn't that fascinating?" She looped her arm in the crook of her daughter's elbow and turned for the elevator.

Lindsay glanced back over her shoulder— silently mouthed, "Sorry!"

Tyler grinned widely, no doubt appreciating her dilemma. He pointed across the lobby. "Meet me in Gretchen's. In twenty?"

She nodded, then dutifully followed her mother.

They entered their suite to find flames crackling in a fireplace and a gorgeous view of Bald Mountain outside sliding glass doors leading to a deck overlooking the rear grounds. Her mother surveyed the layout, the décor, the framed photographs of the famous author. "Such a shame he took his own life," she said, then immediately started in. "You need to change, honey. It's dowdy to meet your fiancé for lunch wearing the clothes you traveled in."

"I'm fine, Mama."

Her mother took her arm and moved her toward the door to the bathroom. "No argument, young lady. You're all wrinkled. Freshen up and I'll pick out something for you to wear."

She could argue. She wasn't a child, for goodness sake. But what was the use? In the weeks leading up to this engagement party, her mother had been acting like a puppy with its tail on fire. It would take a better woman than her daughter to put out the flames.

Besides, she hadn't seen her mama this excited since before Daddy died.

Like a dutiful daughter, she grinned and gave her mother a tight hug. "Oh, all right. I wouldn't want to embarrass anyone by looking dowdy," she said, tongue-in-cheek.

Her mother's face broke into a wide smile. "That's my girl," she said, totally missing the sarcasm in her daughter's voice.

In the bathroom, Lindsay shut the door and pressed her back against it, savoring the first moments she'd had alone in hours.

Truth was, she had not wanted this party. A lavish event of this nature was not her style. When saying so, she'd been quick to learn she was being silly. Both her mom and Tyler insisted an engagement was a big deal, something to be celebrated with fanfare—and with a mere few hundred guests flying in from all over the country.

The DeLuca family came from old money— the kind of wealth that got passed down over many generations. Not necessarily the magnitude of the Kennedys, but close.

"Charles and Sheryl DeLuca have social obligations, Lindsay Kaye," her mother pointed out whenever she risked complaining. "Like your daddy, rest his soul, Tyler is respected in all the right circles and he's a good provider—those are hard to find. Marriage is all about compromise."

Tyler's response wasn't all that different. "Sorry, babe. I know you don't enjoy things like this. Unfortunately, it's expected and we don't really have a choice."

There was little chance of winning this one, not when both her mother and Tyler ganged up on the same side against her. So, Lindsay gave in and let them have their way on this party held clear across the country. She only hoped her wedding next fall wouldn't be too over-the-top.

Lindsay had always pictured herself with someone who loved to nestle up together by a gentle crackling fire and talk about things of the soul. She'd imagined spending Sundays in bed reading—he a crime novel and she a trashy romance with a great happily-ever-after ending. They'd drink cherry colas and eat cheese nibbles without any regard for their yellow stained fingers and the prints they'd leave when turning the pages.

But, then she met Tyler DeLuca.

It was a cold day with an obvious threat of snow, not so unlike the weather outside today. She'd rounded the aisle of a grocery store to find him standing there looking confused and holding two blocks of cheese in this hands.

He looked up at her, a charming and helpless expression displayed across his face. "Hey, do you know the difference between camembert and brie?" he asked.

He was cute. Eyes the color of root beer, and hair to match. An intelligent smile. He wore jeans, loafers and a crisp button-down in her favorite shade of blue, open at the collar.

His confusion, evidenced by his creased forehead, made her amused.

"Well, both brie and camembert are cow's milk cheeses," she explained. "Though one has a higher fat content. Cream is added to brie, giving it a creamier texture."

"Good to know." He nodded and held up the cheese, still looking a bit puzzled. "Second question, how can you know which is which?"

He studied her with disarming intensity as

she laughed, then tried to explain. "Brie is often sold by the slice, a wedge of the larger wheel, while camembert is frequently a whole wheel, unless of course, it's baby brie which is also sold whole." She laughed again, realizing she was rambling a bit. "In other words, good luck."

"Do you have dinner plans?"

The question caught her completely off guard. "What?"

"Let me take you to dinner." He squinted at her, like he could see her mind calculating what to make of him.

The smile left Lindsay's face. "I don't think that's a good idea." She gripped her cart and turned to move on down the aisle.

"Wait—" He reached for her arm. "Don't leave," he pleaded. "I'd like to get to know you better."

Something inside told her to keep moving. She had career plans and no room for a man in her life—at least not right now. Yet her feet wouldn't move. She slowly turned, looked him up and down. "I'd need a name," she challenged.

"A name?"

"Yes, what's your name?"

His eyebrows lifted. "Oh—my name. Of course!" He offered his hand. "I'm Tyler DeLuca."

She knew now the long pause that followed was him checking to see if his name registered, if it had any impact.

It didn't.

"Tyler, huh? I like it." She reached for his hand. "Lindsay Griffin.

They'd ended up at a nearby pizza shop not far from the campus where she attended marketing classes at Wharton. Halfway through their large pepperoni supreme, a rowdy bunch of his friends joined them—fun people she liked a lot.

The evening continued until after midnight, and several pitchers of beer. Despite her initial assessment of Tyler, he was less up tight than she'd first imagined.

At the end of the evening, he offered to walk her home, and against the voice in her head that reminded she didn't know him very well, she let him. Maybe because he was so good-looking, and partly because he seemed to want to so badly.

"I really like your friends," she said, making small talk as they climbed the steps to her brownstone apartment.

"Yeah, they're good guys," he agreed. "But you're the one who made this evening the best I've had in months." His lips curved into something between a smile and outright laughter.

Intrigued, she tilted her head to study him.

That's when he made his bold move. His hands went to each side of her face. Without even asking permission, he leaned in and kissed her— the kind of kiss that made her toes tingle.

They'd seen each other steadily through the remaining few months leading up to graduation, then she returned to Georgia and he to Manhattan and their lives no longer seemed to intersect except by phone or text message.

One crazy night late that following summer she'd been out with friends and returned home to find him in the living room with her mother.

"Tyler, what are you doing here?" she'd asked, surprised at how delighted she was to see him. Her hand went to the band holding her ponytail. "You should have given me a warning. I'd have—"

"Stop. You look beautiful," he told her. Turning to her mother, he added, "Beauty runs in the family."

No southern woman can resist that kind of charm. Mama fell in love with Tyler at that moment, and from then on insisted her daughter was lucky to have done the same. Sometimes in a less than subtle manner—like now.

"Hurry, baby. It's already been ten minutes. You don't want to make Tyler wait."

Lindsay groaned at the sound of her mother's voice coming through the door. "I'll be right out, Mama."

She turned the faucet on, grabbed one of the plush washcloths from the stack and ran it under the warm water. Leaving the water running, she wiped her face. With the other hand, she cracked open the bathroom window and peered out.

A girl and two guys meandered down the sidewalk below. The girl was a little chunky and was wearing what looked like a maid uniform with a jacket over her shoulders. She was laughing and walking arm-in-arm with a guy with a beard who was wearing a ski hat.

A second guy with longer hair walked next to them. "So, we all heading up Baldy after we get off?"

The girl nodded enthusiastically. "Absolutely! We'll meet you up at Seattle Ridge at five. We can get in at least two runs."

The guy with the longer hair glanced up at the window, noticed her and smiled. Embarrassed, Lindsay stepped back out of sight. When she dared peek again, the small group was walking several yards down the sidewalk, still laughing and talking.

Just before they turned the corner, the guy glanced over his shoulder and smiled up at her a second time.

He was cute, in a teddy bear sort of way. His shaggy, light brown hair swept across his broad forehead and he twinkled with good humor. She couldn't look away to save her life. So instead, she took a deep breath and smiled back.

Lindsay eavesdropped on their excited chatter until she could no longer make out their conversation. When their voices had faded, she reluctantly closed the window against the cold, a bit envious of the fun they had planned.

Somehow, her own life had morphed into a regimented task list. She didn't even know that being a bride-to-be could turn into a full-time job. Just picking out the font for the engagement announcements had taken multiple discussions over a two-day period.

Tyler had surprised her by flying into Atlanta for New Year's Eve, a two-carat diamond tucked in his pocket. He presented the ring to her after a dinner of prime rib, roasted potatoes and the perfect pecan pie. She felt both elated and a little nauseous.

Yes, she wanted to marry him. Just not quite this soon.

She'd just graduated college and wanted to foster her coveted career—that of a merchandiser of her own jewelry line. It had been her plan to take a portion of the small trust fund her grandmother left her and travel to Italy. She'd researched and decided to enroll in Alchimia where she'd study under jewelry masters Marzia Rossi and Daniela Boieri who were known for their textile techniques with metal.

A career her mother deemed fine, at least temporarily. "But when you marry, sweetheart— everything changes. Your job will be supporting your husband."

Why couldn't she do both, for goodness sake? This wasn't thirty years ago, when the push between career and family was still a very real struggle. Most women were now expected to have careers, even women in the south.

Lindsay spent years learning marketing and merchandising theories, and wasn't keen on placing her career goals on hold. She'd been certain to make that clear to Tyler from minute one. Besides that, she also intended to travel and experience life before adding parenting to her life resume.

She moved to the mirror and finished washing her face.

With all the engagement party obligations and wedding planning, all her personal plans immediately went on hold. The minute she'd slipped the ring on, her voice didn't seem to matter anymore—not to Tyler, or his parents. And especially not to Mama, a force to be reckoned with who made Scarlett O'Hara look like a wimp.

She was willing to go along for now. But once they were married, she had no intention of neglecting her plans.

Tyler said that's what he loved about her—her quiet spunk.

She thought of the group who had just wandered by, the plans they were making to go skiing. It'd been years since she'd donned a pair of skis and hit the mountainside. The party was being held in one of the premier ski resorts in the nation. Sadly, it was likely she'd get to the end of this celebration weekend without having taken advantage of the slopes.

After she'd changed and was heading out the door to meet Tyler, she stopped and brought the subject up to her mother.

"Mama, remember that time Daddy took us to Connecticut for Christmas and we all went skiing?"

Her mother smiled. "Yes, that was a wonderful holiday. Even though we got laid over in a blizzard in New York and didn't make it home for days." She turned wistful. "I miss your father."

"I'd really like to do that again."

Her mother retrieved a pair of slacks from her suitcase and placed them in the bureau drawer. "Do what, sweet thing?"

"Skiing. I was thinking I'd ask Tyler to go with me."

As soon as she said it, she knew what her mother's response would be, and she wasn't wrong.

"Oh, honey—the schedule is packed as it is. Men like Tyler and his father can't simply change their schedules on a whim. On top of the party and all the entertainment obligations before us, the DeLucas have work commitments that must be attended to. You heard them say some of the guests are business associates."

True. It wasn't easy working for a family business, especially with Charles DeLuca at the helm. Tyler's dad loved to quote John D. Rockefeller, Jr.— *I believe that every right implies a responsibility, every opportunity an obligation, every possession a duty.*

Her mother had her own version of the quote, "The DeLucas are not like other men. A lot of people depend on the business they run. Tyler is not going to be able to drop his responsibilities and entertain you every time you get a whim. In his world, time is money."

"Given that, why did you and the DeLucas decide this party had to be held at a ski resort located on the other side of the country? For goodness sakes Mama, why not just stay on the East Coast?"

Her mother looked at her like she had two heads. "Because, Lindsay, this is *Sun Valley*."

CHAPTER TWO

Skiers just back from the mountain filled the lobby, many wearing bright-colored down parkas and hats lined with fur. With cheeks pink from the cold, the excited tourists chattered about the best way to maneuver moguls, and which was their preferred snow—champagne powder or soufflé dure.

Lindsay wandered through the crowded lobby, envy building yet again. She made a mental note to come back to Sun Valley someday for a vacation, where the only thing pulling at her attention was recreation and having a good time.

Despite knowing it would make her a few minutes late, she'd spent a few minutes in the gift shop admiring jewelry made by local artisans.

Stopping short of pulling out her phone and clicking off a few photos, she made several mental notations of the designs, planning how she might incorporate some of the elements into her own future line.

Before she knew it, time had gotten away from her and now she was fifteen minutes late. If she didn't get a move on, Tyler would be soon be texting.

Now, where was that restaurant?

"Excuse me. Can I help? You look lost."

Lindsay turned to the female voice. "I'm sorry?"

The young woman, who looked remarkably like Princess Kate, offered her hand. "Hi, I'm Karyn Macadam. I'm the hospitality director here at the Sun Valley Lodge. Can I help you find something?"

"Yes, thank you. I'm afraid I can't remember where Gretchen's is located." Lindsay shook the woman's hand, then remembered her manners and introduced herself. "I'm Lindsay Griffin. Soon to be DeLuca."

Delight registered on Karyn's face. "Oh—

you're the big engagement bash."

She nodded. "Yes, that would be us."

"The staff and I have been working hard to make every detail perfect." Karyn's countenance was warm and genial. Lindsay thought they might easily be friends if they lived near one another.

"I hope our mothers haven't made things too difficult," she told her, half cringing.

Karyn grinned and shook her head. "Of course not." She turned for the registration desk and motioned for her to follow. "Let me give you my card. Please, call me anytime you need anything."

"I will." Lindsay smiled warmly and tucked the card in her purse.

Karyn pointed to an area next to the entrance. "And Gretchen's is right over there, near the front door."

Lindsay thanked her and hurried in that direction. She gave the maître d her name and was immediately escorted to meet Tyler, who sat near a massive window overlooking the skating rink.

He folded his linen napkin and rose from the table as she approached. "You're late."

"I know, Babe. I'm sorry. But you know Mama, she insisted I change."

He held her chair for her. "Well, she's been raised to believe appearance matters. And it does."

She took her seat and tucked the linen napkin onto her lap, trying not to let his comment rub. "Okay, my tardiness wasn't entirely Mama's fault," she admitted. "I also dropped into the gift shop for a few seconds. There's these gorgeous pendants, very delicate and—" She paused, realizing she no longer had his attention.

He waved at a couple who was being seated at a table across the room.

"Who's that?" she asked.

"Some of father's business associates here for the party. Jonathan and Dotty Stewart. Oh, they're heading this way."

She smiled in their direction as they approached.

Jonathan Stewart was massive man, well over six feet tall with a hawkish face made more severe by his lack of smile. His wife, on the other hand, was petite and her eyes bubbled with warmth.

She leaned and pulled Lindsay into an embrace. "Well, I finally get to meet the woman who swept Tyler DeLuca off his feet."

"Dotty, don't gush," her husband chastised.

She waved off his comment. "Oh hush, you. This sweet girl is worth gushing over." She reached and lifted Lindsay's hand, examined her engagement ring. "Oh, look at that. Tyler, you chose well. That rock is gorgeous."

Tyler shifted and gave her a crafted smile. "Thank you, Dottie. We're so glad you both could join us to celebrate our engagement."

Dotty took Lindsay's hand, patted it. "I talked to Sheryl last week and we've already started the process for your initiation into the MLS."

"MLS?" she asked.

Tyler placed his arm around her shoulder. "The Manhattan Ladies Society—a philanthropic group of women who lunch once a month."

Dottie nodded enthusiastically. "Oh, yes . . . and we raise a lot of money. Last year, we helped restore the historic Nurolyn Building back to its original grandeur."

Jonathan's stone-like features finally broke into a semi-smile. "Her little effort cost me a fortune. I could have built an entire building for what they were charged."

Dottie didn't seem to mind his veiled insult. "Speaking of historical gravitas," she said. "I love the way this elegant lodge maintains its cultural heritage."

"Yeah, this place is great." Tyler pointed to the far wall. "See those framed photos?"

She nodded.

"Well, that's Gretchen Fraser. She was the first American to win a gold medal in skiing and made her home here in Sun Valley."

"I love it," she said. She reached and folded her hand over his. "Jonathan and I are considering a vacation home here."

"We don't ski, dear," her husband reminded. "And it's time we let these young people enjoy their meal."

She nodded. "Oh, I suppose you're right, dear." She gave them a wistful smile. "Congratulations, and we're looking forward to all the weekend events."

When they were alone and seated again, Lindsay shot Tyler a look. "Please tell me I won't have to lunch with old ladies."

Tyler gave her a wry laugh. "Only once a month."

The waiter approached and handed them menu boards embossed with gold lettering and the sun logo she'd seen everywhere. "I'd also like to point out we are featuring our buffet at this time." He pointed to the linen draped sideboard at the rear of the restaurant laden with silver-plated chafers and trays.

Tyler nodded. "Thank you."

When he'd retreated, Lindsay looked across the table. "Hey, Tyler—let's do something really fun. The party doesn't officially start until Saturday evening. Let's get wild and crazy. I want to go skiing. I'm sure they rent equipment."

His phone dinged, signaling he had a text coming in. He glanced at his phone on the table, scowled. "Sorry, babe. I wish I could but that text just confirmed that Dad and I have a breakfast meeting with some potential clients in the morning." He picked up his menu. "Mr. and Mrs. Michaels to be exact."

Disappointed, she tried to wrap her mind

around what she was learning. "So, how does this work? When you invite potential clients to our engagement party—don't you run the risk of making them feel obligated?"

"May sound tacky, but it's not like that." He placed his menu on the table and patted her hand. "Besides the business relationship, Doreen Michaels also serves on several charities with Mother."

She wanted to say more, but the waiter appeared. After quickly browsing the extensive menu, she ordered an orange and pomegranate salad topped with lobster and Tyler had a Rueben sandwich.

Halfway into their meal, she decided to try again.

"So, my plans to go skiing won't fly. But, I hear there's a little place called the Opera House where they play a complimentary showing of Sun Valley Serenade every evening. Let's go—huh? What do you say?"

His phone rang. He held up his finger and answered. "Sorry. Got to take this," he mouthed as he got up and walked to a corner of the restaurant that provided more privacy.

Discouraged, she pushed her salad plate aside and studied the faces of a couple across the way. The man was nicely dressed, but balding. His wife was superbly coiffed, and carried a diamond on her hand the size of Kentucky. Both sat silent, simply eating.

Granted, it was an old cliché that you can identify the married couple at a restaurant because they're the ones not talking to each other, having long ago run out of things of say. Still, the sight made her uneasy.

Lindsay let out a heavy sigh, watched Tyler talking into his phone and waited.

And waited.

Twenty minutes later, Tyler still had not returned to the table. Lindsay finished her salad.

The waiter reappeared and offered the dessert menu. She declined. He nodded and retreated, but not before he offered to wrap up Tyler's sandwich. "Or, I could bring out a fresh Rueben when Mr. DeLuca returns," he offered.

"No, that's all right. Just leave it. But, thank you."

She fingered her fork, considered her options. Finally, she got up, dabbed the corners of her mouth with the napkin, and walked out.

Tyler didn't seem to notice.

CHAPTER THREE

The sun cast a pink glow across the snow-covered valley as morning dawned over the mountain-jutted horizon. The scene outside Lindsay's hotel window and the private terrace beyond provided the perfect view of Baldy, with its ribbons of white runs threading to the base, yet another reminder of yesterday's disappointments.

Following the scene in Gretchen's, Tyler had found her out by the skating rink, taking in the sun and watching a group of little girls in matching tutus and tights following the lead of their instructor, their little faces tight with concentration.

Her fiancé gently chastised her for leaving the restaurant, but apologized. Even so, his contrition failed to fully erase how often she felt lonely whenever they were together these days—a fact that had kept her awake most of the night.

Beyond the limited amount of time she and Tyler had to spend together, when they did finally connect it seemed they were constantly being pulled in opposite directions. It seemed they had somehow morphed into two people who talked to each other, but no longer communicated. And that frightened her.

Was it normal to have these kinds of thoughts?

* * *

Lindsay glanced over at the bed where her mother slept, wishing she hadn't been railroaded into sharing a room. She stared at the ceiling, thinking about how nice it would be to tune into an old movie, or even turn the lamp on and read.

Knowing she wasn't likely to get any additional sleep, she quietly slipped from her bed and dressed. With as little noise as possible, she opened the door, so as not to wake her mother.

"Lindsay, where are you going?"

She cringed. No such luck. "Go back to sleep, Mama."

"But it's the middle of the night. Where are you going?" she repeated.

"It's morning," Lindsay corrected, not bothering to reveal how early it really was. "I'm heading down for some coffee."

"There's coffee here in the room."

"I know. Sshhh . . . go back to sleep."

Her mother turned over, pulled the fluffy down comforter up over her shoulders. "Well, don't wander far. We have a big day ahead of us," she warned in a muffled voice.

Lindsay sighed. "I know, Mama."

As she slipped from the room into the hallway, a feeling of freedom swept over her.

If lucky, she'd have several hours all to herself, with no one barking expectations her way.

The lodge lobby was nearly empty, except for a young gal behind the registration desk and a doorman who stood at the entrance ready to assist arriving guests not likely to show up at this early hour. In the distance, she could hear the drone of a vacuum.

Near the concierge desk stood a hospitality table, with large silver urns of coffee and platters filled with pastries.

"Those are complimentary," the girl at the registration desk offered from across the room.

"Thanks." Lindsay gave the girl a smile and helped herself to a steaming cup of coffee. Savoring the quiet, she decided to explore.

Even though the gift store was closed at this hour, the glass display window showcased souvenirs, high-end sunglasses and several pieces of gorgeous jewelry. One item in particular caught her eye, A pretty turquoise ring surrounded by tiny pearls set in gold.

She made a note to stop in later and get the name of the artist. She loved studying the methods utilized by master jewelers—hoped to be one herself someday.

She wandered down a hallway leading to the spa and remembered the appointment Tyler's mother had mentioned. She knew her future mother-in-law meant well and appreciated all the effort that had gone into planning this weekend, but once again the details had been planned without so much as consulting with her. Seemed she was being swept up in some big show that had little to do with her and Tyler. At least that's how it felt.

She took a sip of the hot coffee and studied the framed photographs lining the wall. Gary Cooper and Ernest Hemingway chatting circa 1940. Lucille Ball and her children. Marilyn Monroe filming Bus Stop in 1956. And several shots of the Kennedys who frequented the Sun Valley area in the sixties.

She moved on to a framed image of a man poised at the top of a ski hill.

"That's Averill Harriman, the founder of Sun Valley."

Startled, she turned to see a guy standing in an apron. He pulled a net from his head releasing collar-length brown hair that hung in loose waves. His cocoa eyes radiated uncompromising intelligence, yet were filled with amusement. "The resort. It was founded by this guy who wanted to replicate a ski resort he'd visited in Switzerland."

She instantly recognized him as the same guy she'd seen yesterday on the sidewalk below their room. "Yeah?" she replied, noting his warm smile and easy demeanor.

He nodded. "Yup. The dude had his fill of the depression and decided to pursue his dream of providing winter entertainment to the masses. So, in 1936 he opened this lodge, followed by the world's first chairlifts which were installed on Dollar Mountain. That's where Harriman is standing in this photograph." He pointed.

Lindsay leaned in and examined the framed photo more closely, then smiled over at him. "Fascinating. Thank you for sharing."

"No problem," he said. "You here for a ski vacation?"

She sighed, forced her eyes from his and back on another photograph. "I wish."

"What do you mean?"

"It's a long story." She took a sip of her coffee, which was quickly growing cold.

"Well, hey—I'm Jess Barnett." He wiped his palm on his apron and held out his hand. "Sorry, just getting off work."

"Lindsay." She shook his hand. "What do you do? For work, I mean."

A wide grin sprouted on his face. "A lot of things. Like many of us up here, I string together several jobs to fund my ski habit. My main employment gig is here in the kitchen. I'm working my way to sous-chef. Someday I hope to have my own restaurant." He pulled off his apron and folded it. "What about you?"

She hesitated. "I'm a marketing major. Just graduated last spring."

"Really? That's cool. Where do you work?"

"Well, I don't work. I mean, I will—hopefully start my own line of jewelry. But not yet." She held up her left hand. "I'm focusing on my engagement right now." She hated to admit she'd placed her own ambitions on hold in order to make wedding plans. Made her sound like a Jackie Kennedy wanna-be.

Jess let out a low whistle. "Nice rock."

She tucked her hand around her coffee mug. "I plan to start my career after the wedding." She didn't want him thinking she was a total flake, albeit one with money.

Her new friend nodded. "That's cool."

Maybe it was time to divert the subject. "I

think I saw you and your friends yesterday."

"Yeah? I thought that might've been you. We were just off work and heading over to Konditerei for a pastry before we took off up the mountain."

"Sounds wonderful. Skiing, I mean."

"Yeah, it was awesome. Skiing is the next best thing to having wings." His eyes lit up. "Hey, we're heading up the mountain for a couple of runs this morning. You wanna come? The concierge here at the lodge can arrange rental equipment."

Without a minute of consideration, she shook her head no. "I'd love to, but can't. I mean, there's a lot to do. We're here for a big party to celebrate our engagement."

It wasn't right to take off and go skiing without Tyler, was it?

He looked really disappointed. "Oh, I see." As if he sensed her hesitation, he quickly added, "Well, if anything changes and your schedule opens up, we're meeting up on the mountain at nine. Here's my cell."

He rattled off his number and she stored it in her own phone. Why, she didn't know. She couldn't possibly slip away. No doubt, there was an entire list of obligations waiting for her.

"Well, hey—good luck with the wedding and all."

Lindsay nodded, almost wishing she could throw caution to the wind and agree to go. Tyler would be tied up all morning with that business meeting, which meant she'd be left with the *mothers*. How much more planning could go into this event? They'd already considered every detail ad nauseam.

"It was so nice of you to extend an invitation. I wish I had more time," she told him. "I hope you and your friends have fun."

"Yeah, maybe we'll meet up again, huh?"

Ignoring the knot forming in her throat, she nodded. "Yeah, see you around."

A little shaken, and for the life of her she didn't understand why, Lindsay headed back through the lobby to the elevator. Her mother would no doubt be up and wondering where she was by now.

As if on cue, her cell phone dinged and a text message appeared. *Where are you?*

The elevator doors opened. She stepped inside and typed out a reply, then glanced up. The last thing she saw before the doors closed was Jess Barnett standing across the lobby staring after her, smiling.

CHAPTER FOUR

"Where have you been?" her mother scolded the minute she got back to the room. She stood there with face cream on her cheeks, waving her curling iron like it was a weapon. "Our to-do list is a mile long."

Lindsay frowned. "What could that possibly be when the hotel is taking care of everything?"

"That's true to a point, but we have to check with the hotel manager and make sure every detail has been attended to—confirm the seating for the dinner and transport to and from the event. Those are the seemingly little things that can teakettle the entire event if not properly handled. I already sent our clothes down to be pressed. Sheryl made an appointment for us at the spa, but I thought we might nab her and do a little last minute shopping later this afternoon. Pick up anything we might have forgotten to bring." Her mama huffed, looked to the ceiling in frustration. "Oh, why do you argue about everything?"

"Okay, Mama. Settle down. I'm here now, and I'm not arguing about anything." Lindsay sighed, pressed a kiss against her mom's cheek.

A tiny smile sprouted. "I'm sorry. I get a little wound up when so much is at stake."

Lindsay tossed her purse on the sofa table. "Nothing is at stake, Mama. This is a celebration. Despite the fact we're sharing our joy with a few hundred people, this is a time for us to enjoy the moment. Don't you think?"

Her mother wrapped the cord around the curling iron. "Well, yes—of course, Lindsay Kaye. I only worry you fail to totally comprehend your upcoming role in this new family. I was a senator's wife, constantly in the public eye. But you, well you've landed a unique and coveted role in society. Much more will be expected."

Lindsay fought not to roll her eyes. "Mama, I wasn't fishing for fame. I fell in love and got engaged. Any notoriety I enjoy will not come from Tyler, but because of my own accomplishments, whatever they may be."

Her mother waved off the comment. "Oh baby girl, you need to be realistic. You're not going to have time to pursue that little jewelry career of yours after you're married. You'll be far too busy with your obligations, what with all the charity events and foundation boards. You'll have children to raise. Functions to attend."

A mental image of Jonathan Stewart flashed in her mind—the way he'd called his wife's work to restore a building her *little effort*.

"Well, let's take one day at a time, shall we?" She knew she could argue. But what was the point? She'd established long ago that her mother's view of the world and how to live in it differed greatly from her own. She fully intended to make her husband and children top priority, but that didn't necessarily preclude her from pursuing her other gifts and abilities—or perhaps even a morning on the ski mountain.

That's when the idea formed.

A bold move, for sure. But one worth moving on. In part, to make a point, even if in her own mind.

Lindsay fingered her hair. "I talked with one of the kitchen chefs this morning."

Her mother's head perked up. "Oh?"

"Yes. He wanted to show me a few things later this morning so I'll be tied up until early afternoon." The half-truth slipped from her tongue and made her feel like a teenager. Just like back then, she ignored the niggle of guilt. It was better this way. "Can I meet you and Sheryl in the lobby? Say about two?"

Her mother brushed her cheek with a kiss. "Of course, dear. Especially if you're tied up with that chef this morning. I'm so glad to see you being proactive." She motioned for the bathroom. "Now, scoot and get ready. The morning is wasting away as we speak."

* * *

A blast of cold air hit Lindsay's cheeks as she climbed from the gondola. She lifted her face to the sun, a dab of remorse still weighing for sneaking off and not following her mother's prescribed plan. Even so, she was thrilled at the opportunity for a bit of real fun—perhaps the last chance she'd have in the months leading up to her wedding day.

From this vantage point at the top of Bald Mountain, panoramic snowy vistas expanded in all directions. The fresh air so brisk, it almost hurt to breathe.

Her eyes scanned the crowd for a sign of her new friend. Like promised, Jess Barnett stood at the entrance to the Seattle Ridge Day Lodge. He glanced her way and she waved.

With a wide smile, he returned the greeting and hurried to meet her. "Hey, glad you made it. Here let me help you with those." He lifted her skis and poles and hiked them onto his shoulder. "Nice equipment."

"I agree. Wish it were mine." She pulled her ski gloves from her hands and tucked them inside the pockets of her parka.

"Rent it at Pete's?"

She nodded. "I took your advice and contacted the concierge desk. All it took was quick call to Karyn McCadam and she arranged for clothes, equipment—everything."

"Yeah, she's great."

Once again, she was struck by his warm smile and happy spirit. Nothing pretentious.

Walking side-by-side, they traversed the snow-crusted path and made the short distance to the lodge. Jess stored her skis in the rack and held open the door. "C'mon inside. I want you to meet some friends."

Inside, flames crackled in a large fireplace surrounded by groups of comfortable sofas and chairs filled with chattering skiers. Vintage ski equipment and antlered heads decorated the walls leading to a restaurant counter lined with hungry customers responding to the smell of grilled hamburgers and hot chocolate.

Jess led her to a table located near one of the massive windows where two guys and a girl with long brown hair sat. "Hey everybody. This is Lindsay Griffin."

She could barely suppress the feeling of eagerness expanding in her chest. "Hey y'all."

The girl raised her thin eyebrows, laughed.

"Boy, I take it you're from the south."

Lindsay laughed. "Afraid so. Atlanta, Georgia." She extended her hand and shook, deciding she instantly liked this girl. She was like a daisy, bright and cheery, yet sturdy-natured.

"I'm Brooke Ainsley," she said. "And these two goofs are Kyle Lundgren and Abe Menard."

The guy wearing a flannel shirt nodded. "I'm Abe. Glad you could join us." He had a warm smile and sandy-colored hair cut into a style right out of the seventies.

The second guy wore a bandana around his neck. He fingered his beard. "So, Jess tells us you're here in Sun Valley for some big party?"

"And that you're engaged?" Brooke added.

Lindsay slid into a chair and accepted the cup of coffee offered. "Yes, on both counts." She grinned. "I'm afraid our mothers are going a little over the top with the whole thing."

Abe nodded. "Gotcha."

"Thanks for giving me a chance to escape the circus and join you. Goodness, it's beautiful up here."

Brooke tossed a teaspoon of sugar in her

coffee and stirred. "It sure is. Whether you are an adrenaline junkie, or a solitude seeker—this mountain offers exactly what the soul craves. We all live up here in the winter and work just to support our mountain habits."

"We share a place. We all have jobs in the village," Jess explained.

"The village?" she asked.

Brooke picked up her cup. "That's what everyone calls the lodge and the surrounding area with all the shops."

Lindsay nodded. "Got it."

Jess's congenial grin broadened as he waved to more friends sitting across the lodge before returning his attention to the table. "How long do you have before you need to be back?"

She fought back a sigh. "No later than two."

Jess retrieved a ski beanie from his jacket pocket and pulled it onto his head. "We'd best get a run in then."

With that cue, they all drained their cups and rose.

At the ski rack outside, Jess turned to her. "You remember how to do this?"

Lindsay nodded. "I'm hoping it all comes back to me—kind of like riding a bike."

And it was. Following a timid start, she was skiing like a pro in no time.

After an exhilarating run down Gretchen's Gold, they rode the lift to the summit. "Time to experience the real mountain," Jess told her, his eyes sparkling with excitement.

"The real mountain?"

Her new friend winked. "You up for a challenge?"

Lindsay hesitated. She'd proven she remembered how to ride that bike, but from the look on Jess's face, this one had all the signs of being a crotch rocket. She wasn't into thrill rides.

With a light laugh, she tilted her head. "You trying to make me nervous?"

"Not at all," Jess's eyes widened in protest even as he chuckled. "Just checking to see what you are made of." He adjusted the zipper on his jacket. "But don't let that scare you. You're safe with me."

Brooke stabbed her poles into the snow. "Don't believe it. Rumor has it Jess made a girl cry once."

Lindsay looked at him in mock horror. "You made someone cry?"

"Okay, admittedly she was in the third grade and was scared to go down the slide on the playground."

"So you pushed her," Brooke accused. "PS—I was that girl."

Lindsay laughed. "And you remained friends?"

The girl shrugged. "Jess is hard to toss aside. Kind of like a candy bar you know you shouldn't eat, but you do anyway because he's so darn sweet."

"Are you two going to continue this chit-chat?" There was a gleam in Jess's eyes. "Or, are we going to give Lindsay the good time we promised?"

She felt a trickle of excitement run down her spine. Her eyes met his own. "Let's do it!"

Minutes later, she was poised alongside her new friends at the crest of Easter Bowl, a run designated for advanced skiers.

Brooke adjusted her goggles. Kyle plugged a

set of earbuds inside his ears and pressed a button on his tiny iPod and tucked it deep inside this jacket before zipping up.

Abe punched the snow with his poles. "You're going to love this. The pow is going to be great. Then you'll hit a bit of corduroy before the lane turns to six-inch crud. Can be a little unpredictable from there, so just follow us."

She nodded, despite feeling a sudden case of nerves, and not knowing half of what he was talking about.

For the briefest of moments, the sour taste of panic rose in her throat. She'd skied often with her father when he was alive, even got competent at the sport when he'd take her to upper state New York for extended weekends. He'd died over six years ago, and she hadn't clicked the bindings on a pair of boots since. Not until today.

The first run had been fairly easy, one meant for near beginners. But this course would take every ounce of skill she could muster.

Her eyesight blurred. She began to hyperventilate, and her calves shook. She looked over at Jess. He gave her a thumbs up.

Awkwardly, stiff with sudden fear, she gazed at the drop, the glittering white blanket bordered by pine trees, their spidery branches heavily laden with ice.

The only place to go was down.

Kyle and Abe took off first. They hurtled down the groomed fall line, then diverted into a deeper area that had not been groomed. Instantly, they were lost from view except for the tops of their hats. Brooke followed.

Jess looked her way, gave her a quick nod and he too plummeted down the run, following after his friends.

Lindsay took a deep breath, tipped her skis over the ledge and dropped in beside him. And kept dropping. Everything disappeared—the sky, the trees, and even her hands were suddenly hidden in a sea of white. The powder was deeper than anything she'd experienced, and for a second she couldn't tell if she were moving or if she'd stalled in a snowdrift.

Seconds later, she felt her legs beneath her, her skis flying on autopilot. Two turns, then three—all under a blanket of frozen white until she gained enough momentum to broach the surface. And not a moment too soon as a wave of airborne powder flew over her helmet.

Her heart raced with exhilaration.

It was true what she'd read—skiing pow was like swimming through a white sea. You're in it, and it's in you.

Lindsay hooted with giddiness.

Suddenly, her skis broke through and she landed on corduroy—snow that had been groomed leaving tiny grooves that resembled its namesake fabric.

She picked up speed, raced down the slope.

Swish—glide—swish!

This was what she'd so missed—the closest feeling to flying she'd ever experienced.

She could feel her daddy's presence, hear him egg her on. *"Sit back on the tails of your skis, sweetheart. It'll give you much better balance and stability."*

She lengthened her turns, swinging broad and wide, letting the sun warm her face and her soul.

Several yards later, she hit another change in snow surface. As predicted, the corduroy turned to crud which made her work harder to maintain her speed and balance. She gripped the poles tighter, pushed against the skis surface a little harder, made tighter turns.

Across the lane, Kyle veered dangerously close to the tree line. She could see him laughing as he tucked and gained speed. He straightened just as he hit a pile of snow that launched him airborne.

He glided through the air and landed without wavering. Clearly, he'd maneuvered that jump more than once.

For the next minutes, everything in the world was right. Far before she was ready, the run was over. She plowed to a stop at the base of Olympic Ridge, joining the others.

Lindsay couldn't help herself as she raised from unhooking the bindings and stepped from her skis. She flung her arms around Jess's neck. "Thank you! That was wonderful!"

From the side, Kyle pulled his buds out of his ears just as Abe chimed in. "Like sex for your feet!"

Brooke slapped his chest with her gloves.

"You're in mixed company."

Lindsay turned to Jess. "I mean it. I haven't had that much fun since—well, since I don't remember when."

A look passed between them. She noticed something in his eyes she rarely recognized. *He saw her.*

Not the person she was expected to be, but the essence of her—what she longed for and what fed her spirit, what made her genuinely happy.

The look in his eyes was so intense she felt compelled to glance away.

"Again, I don't know how to thank y'all for such a wonderful time," she muttered, now feeling a bit flustered. "This morning will be a memory I'll treasure for some time."

She hugged Abe, Kyle and Brooke, jealous of their life-long connection and the closeness they enjoyed. She wished she could spend much more time with these people.

She turned to Jess last. Without waver, she lifted the palm of her hand and cupped his cheek. "Thanks, Jess. I had a ball."

And with that, she was gone.

CHAPTER FIVE

Jess watched as Lindsay handed off her equipment to the driver and climbed on board the shuttle. Before disappearing inside, she turned and wiggled her fingers in their direction. He waved back and followed her through the windows until she found a seat.

"What's this?" Brooke asked.

He turned. "What?"

Abe slapped his shoulder. "That. You're like a puppy dog in heat. I swear your tongue hit the ground when she reached and touched that ugly mug of yours."

Jess scowled. "You're off base. The lady's engaged."

Kyle pulled his cap from his head. "Tell that

to your face, man."

Brooke shook her head. "Sorry, Jess. I haven't seen that look since Jenny Martin in the fourth grade."

"Who?"

"Jenny Martin. The little blonde girl who beat you at kick ball, pushed you down and kissed you."

He gave her a dirty look. "Stop. You've got it all wrong. Both on Jenny what-ever-her-name-was and on this gal."

"Lindsay."

"Yes, Lindsay. There's nothing brewing in the hot zone there, I promise you."

Even as he said it, he knew the statement wasn't exactly true. There was something about this girl. He couldn't quite put his fingers on what made him feel so protective, but whenever she was around he wanted nothing more than to see her happy.

Problem was, she was taken. Like about to get married taken.

That was just his kind of luck.

CHAPTER SIX

The shuttle pulled under the porte-cochere and came to a stop. The driver swung the doors open wide and the passengers, including Lindsay, stood and made their way to the front of the shuttle. Still on a mental high from her morning on the mountain, Lindsay followed the crowd and descended the couple of steps, then moved for the front doors of the Sun Valley Lodge.

Karyn Macadam stood just inside the entrance. "You're back! Did you have a nice time?"

"Oh my, yes. I'd forgotten just how much I love to ski. The snow was in perfect condition. And the views! The views from up there are—well, like a bit of heaven. She leaned close and lowered her voice. "After the wedding, I suspect we'll be visiting the area often, given my future in-laws have a place in Sun Valley. I plan for us to return and hit the slopes every year."

"That's what we like to hear. Don't worry about your equipment. I'll take care of everything. By the way, your mother and your handsome guy have been looking for you." Karyn gave her a conspiratorial smile. "I told them I hadn't seen you since early this morning."

Lindsay smiled. "Great, that's perfect. Thank you."

"No problem. I think your group is waiting for you in the Duchin Lounge."

"Okay, thanks."

Lindsay headed that way, then realized she needed to freshen up a bit and turned for the elevator.

"Hey, where've you been?" Her fiancé's voice stopped her in her tracks.

She pivoted and tucked a stray strand that had fallen from her ponytail behind her ear. "Hi, babe!" she said, a little too brightly.

Puzzled, Tyler glanced outside the door at the shuttle and repeated his question. "Where'd you go? We've been waiting lunch for you."

"I'm sorry." She hesitated, not wanting to tell an untruth. That was no way to start a marriage. Honesty between a man and wife was critical. "Okay, time to confess. I knew you were tied up all morning, so I snuck off and went skiing."

"Alone?"

She tilted her head to meet his eyes. "No. I met some people and they invited me."

As if a switch had been thrown, his warm smile molded into an icy stare. "With strangers?"

She shook her head. "Of course not—I mean, yes. They were strangers, until I met them. But they weren't strangers when I agreed to go skiing." She knew she was rambling, but seemed unable to stop. "Their names are Jess, Brooke, Kyle and Abe. You'd really like them, I think."

Tyler scowled. "Who are these—people? Guests?"

She swallowed. "Not exactly. They work for the lodge."

The look on his face said it all. Her fiancé could be a bit of a snob.

"Oh, there you are." Her mother's sing-song

voice floated across the lobby.

Thankful for the interruption, Lindsay broke gaze with Tyler and moved to hug her mama. "Yes, and I'm sorry I held you all up. But I'm here now, so let's get some lunch. Shall we?"

She locked arms with her mother and headed in the direction of the Duchin Lounge, fully aware Tyler was still staring after them.

Inside, his family was seated in plush leather club chairs around a marble-topped table at the back of the room.

"There you are!" Tyler's mother stood and gave her a tight hug. "We ordered for you dear. A shrimp salad."

Her mama motioned for to sit, then took her own seat and folded her pressed linen napkin across her lap. "I know shrimp's not your favorite, honey. But dress fittings are right around the corner and all the other selections were laden with calories."

Her future father-in-law waved Tyler closer. "Son, sit." He looked to his wife. "Remember that time your father talked me into investing in that shrimp boat?" He laughed. "Lost my shirt."

Sheryl waved off his comment. "Oh, you never went into that deal for the money and you know it. You bought the vessel from Daddy's war buddy, as a favor."

"What are you talking about, dear? A good businessman does everything to make money," Charles teased.

Lindsay reached for her glass of water. "I can certainly see why you both love it here in Sun Valley. I snuck off and went skiing this morning and fell in love with the slopes, the views, the fresh air—well, all of it."

"By yourself?" Tyler's mother looked confused.

"She went with some people she met," Tyler said, answering for her. He glanced at his watch. "But I thought you ladies wanted to talk wedding plans."

Sheryl and her mother exchanged excited glances.

His mother dabbed her napkin at the corner of her mouth. "Yes, we have a lot to consider. This weekend's engagement party is the launch of several months leading up to what will no doubt be a social event that people will be talking about for a long time."

Lindsay cringed. She'd been naïve to hope for an understated ceremony without a lot of fanfare.

Sheryl motioned for a waiter, then reached in her bag and pulled out what looked to be a planner. Lindsay recognized the leather pattern, had seen it in a magazine her mother often read—a Trish McEvoy. Sheryl pulled two identical planners and handed one to Lindsay and her mother. "I've recorded all the wedding events and corresponding dates for us."

"Oh, here we go," Charles jingled the ice in what looked to be a glass of bourbon. Or, maybe scotch.

He caught where she was looking. "Poppy Van Winkle—aged fifteen years."

Lindsay nodded and made a mental note. She couldn't imagine trying to buy this man a gift and that might be an item he'd appreciate on future birthdays.

Sheryl looked across the table. "You boys enjoy your drinks, but you need to listen up. These plans involve both of you as well."

It was Tyler's turn to laugh. "Everyone at this table knows you ladies are going to make all the decisions and we're going to show up when and where you tell us to. Right, Dad?"

"Well, stated." Charles caught the look from his wife. "And we're happy to do it," he added.

Lindsay wished she could state the same, and say it truthfully. In reality, she wished she was still up on Baldy. She'd take the thrill of racing down the slopes over this discussion any day.

The waiter arrived at the table and Sheryl ordered another glass of wine. "Anyone else?"

Her mother ordered a glass of chardonnay. "You want something, dear?"

Lindsay shook her head no, opened her planner and scanned the pages. Goodness, how many teas was she being forced into, anyway?

She flipped another page, frowned. "Uh, I see you have a meeting with the event planner scheduled on the same day I'm registered for an international gem and jewelry show in Atlanta. One of the designers is a highly regarded artisan I've followed for some time. I'd hoped to meet privately with her, pick her brain a bit."

Tyler folded his hand over hers. "That's great, babe." His attention was pulled to the television mounted behind the bar. "Dad, looks like the Giants are out of the playoffs again this year."

"Honey." Her mother didn't bother to hide her impatience. "Sheryl snagged Phillipa Tarrant. Do you have any idea how lucky we are to even get on her calendar? I mean, there's simply no question this is a priority over anything else."

Tyler's mom chimed in. "I'm afraid your mother's correct, honey. We can't just stand her up and ask her to reschedule. It's just not done. I'm sorry."

Lindsay looked to Tyler for support. He bailed on her and simply shrugged.

She took a deep breath, tried to temper the tone of her response. "Well, of course. If the meeting can't possibly be rescheduled."

Her mother hugged her shoulder. "That's my girl."

Sheryl clasped her hands with excitement. "Okay, now to the particulars. Phillipa has arranged for a private showing with both the Martina Liana and Alfred Sung collections."

She felt her mother squeeze her knee under the table. Her eyes glistened with excitement.

"I talked with Charles and we recommend an elegant reception dinner at the Cipriani on 42nd, especially given that we've booked the actual wedding venue at The Plaza."

Her mother looked like a three-year old sitting in front of a Christmas tree loaded with wrapped packages waiting to be opened. "The Plaza is where Michael Douglas married Catherine-Zeta Jones."

How did her mom even know this stuff?

Charles wiped the bottom of his glass with a tiny paper napkin engraved with the Sun Valley logo. "It took a couple of calls, but the management opened up a Saturday evening for us. Middle of June—perfect weather."

Sheryl nodded. "June is a busy month and doesn't give us much time."

Lindsay's brows lifted. "We—uh, we're holding the ceremony in June?"

Tyler squeezed her hand. "You don't mind, do you babe? I know we talked about fall, but—"

Her mother piped up. "Of course we don't mind. Everything you've arranged sounds absolutely perfect!"

Lindsay thought her mother had lost her ever-loving mind. Did she have any idea how much all this was going to cost?

As if reading her mind, Charles put the matter to rest. "We certainly hope you'll grant us the privilege of sharing the cost with you, Julia."

Sheryl placed her hand on her mother's arm. "Oh, yes. We'll have a guest list heavily laden with business clients. It's only right that we share the burden of the cost."

"Well, that's not necessary," her mama replied. "But, if you insist."

Lindsay couldn't believe what she was hearing. Even at a shared cost, the budget for an event like this was over-the-top expensive and certainly far beyond any budget her mother could sensibly bear.

This was crazy! She didn't even *want* all this. She'd much rather have a simple ceremony followed by a quiet dinner somewhere nice.

She started to say so, but her mother cut her

off before she could speak. "Lindsay and I love these plans!"

The comment urged Sheryl on. "Oh, good. On the next page of your planner, you'll see the menu Phillipa is recommending. Chevre and potato millefeuille, followed by syrah short ribs with crispy fried shallots or a pistachio-crusted halibut. Dessert will be a three-deck white wedding cake with vanilla buttercream, chocolate fudge and chocolate truffle granache—which will be cut during the reception to Marvin Gaye's *'How Sweet it is to be Loved by You.'*"

Tyler picked up his drink. "Make sure we have an authentic Japanese sushi bar set up for hor d'oeurves." He leaned over to her. "Wait until you see the guest list. Dad talked with Wolf Blitzer last week and was assured he and his lovely wife would be there."

Tyler had always been a fan of the CNN anchors. She suspected he'd wanted to go into television news reporting, but had acquiesced to his father's wishes for his son to share in the family brokerage. Unlike her, her fiancé loved being the center of attention.

Her phone dinged. She reached and pulled it from inside her bag and swiped the front face. A message popped into view.

Hey, we really enjoyed the time with you up on the mountain this morning. A few of us are getting together at our house tonight. Nothing fancy. Just burgers and beers. You wanna come? Seven o'clock. Text me and I'll give you directions. Oh, and you can bring your guy if you want.

Lindsay's heart pounded with elation. That was the most fun thing she'd heard about in the last hour. She poised her thumbs to tap out that she'd be there.

"Honey?"

Her mother's voice pulled her attention back to the table.

"Lindsay, honey—did you hear Sheryl? She asked if you'd rather have rib-eyes or prime rib tonight."

"Tonight?"

Tyler leaned back in his club chair to allow the server to place his lunch plate on the table in front of him. "Yeah, you remember. Mom and Dad are hosting the early guests who have arrived for our engagement party."

Lindsay scanned past discussions in her mind for some trace of the expected appearance. None came to memory. Even so, she pasted a smile. "Of course." She turned to her future mother-in-law. "I love prime rib."

"Then prime rib it is!"

Lindsay looked at her phone. With a sigh of disappointment, she closed out the message. She'd just have to tell Jess and his friends she couldn't come.

CHAPTER SEVEN

As one might expect, the DeLucas' vacation home was a showplace, impeccably decorated with soaring raw timber ceilings and windows overlooking the Bigwood golf course. Their place was within walking distance of the Sun Valley Lodge, but due to the outdoor temperatures, Tyler drove Lindsay and her mother to the party.

They parked and Tyler helped her mother from the backseat of the four-wheel-drive Jeep he'd borrowed from his dad. "Careful, Julia. It can get really slick out here."

She took his hand, smiled broadly in his direction. "Thank you, Tyler." She surveyed his parents' house. "This is an amazing location."

"Yeah, Dad golfs. Mom can watch him tee

off while she drinks her morning coffee on the deck. Sadly, they don't often spend much time here in the summer and the house sits empty. Mom prefers the Hamptons."

Inside, a crowd much larger than Lindsay had anticipated had already assembled. Goodness, if these were the guests who had arrived early, how many would be attending the big engagement party tomorrow night?

Lindsay and her mother were introduced to several pockets of family friends and associates. Tyler offered to take her mother on a tour of the house. She quickly accepted, leaving her with Mr. and Mrs. Billingsley, an older couple who Tyler confided owned major real estate holdings across the nation, with most located Boston.

"So, you're Lindsay!" The tight-faced woman folded her purple-veined hands over top of hers. "Charles and Sheryl have been boasting about the smart girl their Tyler is marrying. You are simply lovely, dear." She turned to her white-haired husband. "Isn't she lovely, Harrison?"

He leaned forward. "What was that, dear?"

She smiled patiently and repeated her question. "I said, isn't she lovely?"

He nodded, lifted a bacon-wrapped shrimp from a tray and looked the pretty white-gloved server up and down. "Oh my, yes."

The woman placed her hand on her husband's arm. "No, Harrison—this is Tyler's fiancé." She redirected him and he smiled up at Lindsay. "Oh, goodness. Yes, this one is pretty too."

Lindsay extricated herself from the conversation as politely as possible, delighted to note a group of women standing by the fireplace were more near her age.

She joined them, with hand extended. "Hi, everyone. So very glad you could join us this weekend."

One of the women smiled and shook her hand. "Hi, I'm Candace. It's really nice to meet you, Lindsay."

Following introductions, one of them—an elegant-looking blonde named Elise—stepped forward, wine glass in hand. "So, you're the one who caught Tyler DeLuca." She grinned. "Well played."

Another girl wearing a cashmere sweater in a

pretty shade of aqua and matching heels quickly echoed the same sentiment. "Do you know how many have chased after that man? Unsuccessfully, of course. By the way, I'm Angela."

A fourth woman with a long ponytail and diamond earrings the size of small marbles agreed. "We've all tried to fix him up. So, tell us, how'd you do it?"

Lindsay didn't know what to say. She decided to play along with her new razor-boned friends who obviously ate next to nothing and spent a good deal of time at the gym. "Well, it took a big net and several neighbors to hold him down."

The woman named Elise laughed. "I reiterate—well played."

Over the next minutes, she learned the fourth woman was named Belinda, but everyone called her Bibby. Lindsay couldn't help but think she'd personally have preferred to use Belinda. Bibby sounded like something you'd name a cat.

In stark contrast to her own childhood where she walked to and from school with a pack of mixed-age neighborhood kids every morning, then played kick ball in the street and mucked around backyards until called in for dinner, she learned each one of these women were raised by nannies in uberwealthy and status-conscious neighborhoods, their mothers glossy and moneyed and privileged.

In turn, they'd raised their own families on the Upper East Side, their days filled with drivers and nannies and helicopter rides to the Hamptons. There were the "right" music classes for two-year-olds, tutors for three-year-olds to prep them for kindergarten entrance exams and interviews, and playdate consultants for four-year-olds who didn't know how to play because they didn't have time to play because they had so many "enrichment classes"—French, Mandarin, Little Learners, as well as golf, tennis, and voice lessons—after preschool.

There were wardrobe consultants to help these moms buy the right clothes and birthday parties that cost $5,000 and up in apartments so big and with ceilings so high that they could have full-sized indoor bouncy castles inside.

Lindsay's heart pounded as she tried to take it all in. She smiled at what she hoped was appropriate times. She nodded and asked polite follow-up questions, hoping she didn't stumble in this game of high-stakes jockeying.

Over the next minutes, the women continued to talk—their words pounding into her consciousness like sledge hammers.

Surgical dimple augmentation . . . BollyX workouts . . . bonus achievements.

Elise stopped talking, stared at her. "Lindsay, are you all right?"

"What? Uh, yeah. I'm fine." Sweat sprouted across her brow. "I mean, I think I—uh, would y'all excuse me a minute?"

Frantically, she glanced around the room. Her breath was coming faster now. She knew to shut her eyes, breathe deeply. Instead, she managed to eek out, "Does anyone know where the bathroom is?"

That earned her sympathetic looks from each of the women. Bippy—Biddy—or, whatever her name was, pointed down a hallway.

Lindsay felt panic rise in her throat. A familiar gray fog rolled into her line of sight. She raced in the direction of the hallway and felt her way to an open door, quickly tucked inside and shut the door behind her, locked it.

Her hands found their way to the faucet and she turned on the water—splashed some across her face, ignoring the desperate act would no doubt ruin her make-up.

The air was so hot, thick. She needed to breathe.

Someone knocked on the door. Lightly, then more insistent.

"Lindsay, honey? It's me, Tyler. Let me in."

She turned, filled her lungs with much needed air, and unlocked the door.

Tyler pushed himself through and locked the door behind him. "Babe? What's the matter? Elise came and told me she thought you were sick."

Lindsay grabbed the cold marble counter top and hung on.

"Lindsay, are you all right?" There was real concern in his voice.

She held up a hand, squeezed her eyes shut and deliberately forced a slow breath in, a long slow breath out.

In . . . out. In . . . out.

"Babe?"

"I'm—I'm okay," she tried to tell him.

His hand went to her shoulder. "You don't look okay."

She buried her head in his chest, fighting back instant tears. "Tell me something," she whispered against his tie.

He kissed the top of her head.

She sniffed. "Do I get a bonus?"

Tyler pulled back. "A what?"

She looked at up at him, miserable. "A *bonus*."

She'd been thunderstruck to hear Elise, Angela and Betty Boop talk about their annual wife bonuses. Angela, who didn't have an outside job, mentioned she would buy a table at an upcoming event once her bonus was set. Elise, a woman with a business degree but no job mentioned waiting for her "year-end" to shop for clothing.

Seeing her reaction, they'd boldly explained a wife bonus might be hammered out pre-nup or post-nup and would be distributed not only how well her future husband's funds had done but her own performance—how well she managed the home budget, and her weight, whether their future children got into a "good" school—the same way their husbands would be rewarded with business profits.

These women claimed the bonuses were their tickets to financial independence and participation in a social sphere where you don't just go to lunch, you buy a $10,000 table at the benefit the friend is hosting.

Lindsay's lip quivered. "Answer me. Do you intend to give me a wife bonus?"

Tyler's fingers lifted her chin. "Honey, you're being silly to worry. I wouldn't call the money a bonus, but of course you'll have access to discretionary funds to use how you see fit. You'll be my wife."

He handed over her purse. "You might want to freshen up a bit. Maybe reapply your lipstick."

Numb, she nodded and took her bag from his hands.

"You okay now?" he asked.

She refrained from scowling. Instead, she pasted a purposeful smile. "I think so."

"That's good to hear. Look, hon—I need to get back to our guests. Don't be long, okay."

She assured him she would join him shortly.

As soon as the door shut behind him, she sunk onto the floor, dug inside her purse for her phone.

Determined, her thumbs worked the keyboard.

"Thanks for the invite. Give me the directions and I'll see you in a few."

CHAPTER EIGHT

Tyler pulled up in front of a tiny house and wedged the Jeep between a snow bank and a pickup truck with a gun rack in the rear window and mud flaps. "Nice place," he said as he cut the engine. "Is that a sofa on the porch?"

"Wrong house," Lindsay corrected, pointing to the place next door. "That's where the party is."

Tyler didn't say anything. He didn't need to, his eyes said it all for him.

Lindsay cleared her throat. "You didn't have to come."

"No, no—I wanted to, uh—meet your friends," he tried to assure her, though not very convincingly.

Minutes later, they stood at the entry to a

small house with a gabled roof and shutters. Potted arborvitae loaded with white lights stood on either side of a door painted glossy black with a little painted welcome sign hanging prominently in the center.

Before she knocked, she glanced over at Tyler. "Is that a neon beer sign hanging in their window?" he asked, still fascinated with the house next door.

Lindsay sighed, took a deep breath and pounded on the door—loud enough to be heard over the music coming from inside the house.

No answer.

She pounded again and suddenly, the door opened.

"You made it." Jess greeted them with a wide smile. "C'mon in." He motioned them inside and extended his hand. "You must be Tyler."

Tyler nodded and shook. "Yes. Her fiancé."

"Yeah, man. Congratulations. I'd take your coats but you'll need 'em. The party's out back."

Brooke and Abe made their way toward them from the tiny kitchen area, their hands filled with bags of chips.

"Hey, Lindsay. So cool you could make it." Brooke leaned and gave her a hug, then turned to Tyler. "You must be the lucky guy. So glad you could make the party."

Abe shifted the chip bags and offered up a free hand.

Tyler gave him a less than enthusiastic handshake. "Yes, thanks for including us."

Jess pretended not to notice and motioned for them to follow. "Well, like I said, the party's out back."

Tyler and Lindsay followed him out a sliding glass door and onto a small covered wooden deck where several people milled around chatting. Several more huddled around flames extending from a fire pit located in the center of the small yard. Despite its humble size, the yard had a festive look.

"Oh my goodness, this is beautiful," Lindsay exclaimed. "Wow."

Brooke's face lit up. "You like it? I had to push the guys to let me drape strings of lights along the fence, but they finally gave in."

Lindsay couldn't hide her astonishment. The

scene was worthy of a pinning on Pinterest. "I especially like the way you wrapped the bare tree limbs with white twinkly lights. Really pretty."

"Well, hey. Let's get you guys something to drink." Jess looked to Tyler. "Beer?"

Tyler nodded. "Sure. Have any Guinness? Or, perhaps a LaBatt?"

Jess shook his head. "Sorry, Coors Light or Bud. Maybe a stray Micholob." He bent to a cooler that had seen better days, lifted the lid and scrounged in the ice. "Nope. Just Coors or Bud."

Lindsay intercepted the discussion. "We'll both have a Coors."

Tyler gave her a bit of a look. "Yeah, Coors is fine." He took the offered can, popped the top and drew a long and healthy drink. "Mmm . . . Colorado Kool-aide."

An uncomfortable silence followed.

Lindsay cleared her throat. "Who are all these people?" she said, steering the subject to a topic that didn't include imported beer, or the lack thereof.

Jess slapped the palm of his hand against his forehead. "So much for good manners. Sorry—"

He stepped forward. "Hey, everybody. This is Lindsay Griffin, a friend of mine. And Tyler—uh, sorry?"

Her fiancé straightened and nodded to the others. "DeLuca. Tyler DeLuca." He paused, waited for the recognition his family name normally garnered. Getting none, he scowled and took another drink of beer.

"Nice to meet everyone," Lindsay said with bright enthusiasm, partly to make up for Tyler's lack of the same.

Originally she'd planned to come alone, been halfway to the taxi waiting at the curb when her phone rang. She looked down at the caller ID, a smiling Tyler staring back. She hadn't wanted to answer. But, of course she did.

"Hey," he said when she picked up. "Where are you?"

She kept her eyes straight ahead, fixed on the taxi. She didn't want to make this hard. "I—I'm leaving."

"You're what?"

"I should have told you. And I'm sorry, but those conversations in there. Well—I needed to get away."

"Where are you going?" he demanded, yet already she could sense the worry in his voice, knew he was tempering his response. "You want to tell me what's going on?" he asked. "This isn't like you."

And that was the problem in a nutshell. None of this was her really. And especially not the *fly into Sun Valley for the announcement party*—which was silly really, because nothing was being announced. Everyone attending already knew they'd gotten engaged. Most had seen the ring, and had gushed over the size and brilliance of the stone.

Lindsay sighed. She was rambling—even inside her head.

She'd done her best to explain, knowing fully Tyler would likely be unable to understand her feelings. Yet, he'd done his best, she supposed.

"No, if that's what you want to do," he said. "Then I'll come with you."

She loved Tyler. She did.

But that didn't mean she didn't wrestle with all that marrying him would mean, in terms of changes to her life. She wished for a way to slow everything down a bit. They needed time to sort out what they wanted—not what his parents pushed them into, or what her mother hoped for, or what his job demanded.

Even more, she did not intend for her life to mimic those of the women she'd met earlier this evening. She didn't want to be accused of judging their personal choices, but those lifestyles did not reflect her own aspirations.

When she said *"I do"* it would be to a man who desired to create and share a life of their own making—one that made them *both* feel secure and happy. Tyler needed to understand that.

She took a drink of her beer and smiled over at Jess, hoping to convey her unspoken appreciation for him being so nice. Especially given Tyler's pitiful reciprocation.

He smiled back at her, holding her gaze as if to say not to worry about it.

Finally, he cleared his throat. "How about some tunes?"

The suggestion met with hardy approval from those gathered around the fire.

"Great, I'll grab my guitar," he said.

Lindsay turned to Brooke. "Jess plays?"

Her new friend nodded. "Oh, yeah. We all do. We play every other weekend at the Whiskey Jacques." She asked them to excuse her and disappeared inside.

Tyler leaned in her direction, whispered, "And they play in a bar? Classic."

She nudged him with her elbow. "Sshh . . . someone will hear you."

Kyle bent and tossed another log on the fire, sending a shower of sparks into the darkness overhead. Brooke returned with a guitar, handed it to Jess.

Jess carried the instrument to an empty lawn chair and sat. He positioned his fingers on the frets, strummed a few chords. He paused and adjusted the tuning pegs, then smiled in her direction from across the fire and began playing.

Lindsay recognized the tune almost immediately—Led Zeppelin's *Stairway to Heaven*.

Brooke grabbed a beer from the cooler and joined them. She leaned close. "Jess is a seventies music aficionado. This is his favorite song."

Lindsay sighed. "One of mine, too."

As the hauntingly tender melody played, Lindsay found herself looking up into the dark sky, appreciating the thousands of twinkling stars. The inky canopy looked like someone had taken a pin to velvet and indeed, heaven itself was shining through.

Lindsay couldn't help but continue to stare, mesmerized. It made her feel like something bigger was watching over them and everything would end up right with the world.

She glanced around, wondering where Tyler had taken off to.

Laughter pulled her attention back to the scene around the campfire. A girl with long blonde hair stood at the beer cooler with Tyler next to her.

Despite the cold temperature, she wore a tight-fitting sweater so thin you could make out the line of her bra underneath. Immediately, Lindsay's internal meter went on high alert. Not because of what she was wearing, but because she was now leaning against Tyler and whispering something in his ear. He laughed, seeming to be tickled with whatever the blonde had said.

Inside, Lindsay's gut tightened. She knew what was going on with this gal—and she didn't like it. Even more, she didn't like how Tyler failed to create some distance.

Brooke saw it too.

Lindsay moved in the direction of her fiancé, paced her steps steadily, trying to make her thoughts match.

"Hey, Tyler—who's your new friend?" She didn't try to hide the challenge in her eyes as she drilled the blonde with a pointed look.

"Oh, darn!" The girl formed her lips into an exaggerated pout. "You're taken." She sighed heavily, as she no doubt noticed the ring on Lindsay's finger. "All the cute ones are."

That didn't stop her from giving Tyler a lusty grin. She pressed her considerable assets against his arm as she moved aside. "If you ever change your mind, you have my number."

* * *

Jess closed his eyes and sang the words to his favorite song. Even with his eyes shut, an image of

Lindsay formed. No doubt, the girl was beautiful. The way her eyes twinkled when she smiled, and those dimples that formed on either side of her mouth. And the way she smelled every time he stepped close.

Too bad she was off limits.

He shook the thoughts from his head and focused on the words to the song. The meaning of the lyrics was not lost on him, that money couldn't buy the important things in life. Funny how this once he found himself wishing he had more to offer, that he could compete with rich boy over there.

He strummed the notes ending the first interlude, opened his eyes.

Suddenly, there was a commotion over near the beer cooler. Some girl he didn't even know, a friend of a friend of Kyle's, was pushing herself up against Lindsay's fiancé, who seemed to be enjoying the encounter.

Out of the corner of his eye he caught Lindsay walking that way, every step measured.

While he hadn't known her long, he knew she was a class act. Still, what was about to go down wasn't going to be good.

Lindsay said something.

The blonde tossed back her head, laughed.

Jess stopped playing. He stood and handed off his guitar to Brooke. "Here, take this."

* * *

Lindsay glared in astonishment. "You took her number?"

Tyler threw up his hands in surrender. "Hey, she was coming onto me—not the other way around."

Lindsay narrowed her eyes, mentally calculated the number of martinis he'd had at his parents, then added the several beers he'd downed here.

He dropped his arm around her shoulder and moved to kiss her.

She pulled back. "You smell like a brewery."

"Take it easy, Lindsay," he said, his words slurring slightly. "It's not like I was unfaithful."

Unfaithful. What a word choice. As if there were only one way to make someone lose faith.

"Besides." He straightened. "You've been

playing twinkle eyes all night with Guitar Boy."

She cleared her throat, purposefully lowered her voice. "Excuse me?"

Jess appeared. "Hey, everything all right?"

Tyler gave him a shove. "Move on. This is none of your business."

Lindsay gasped in horror—watched as her fiancé balled his fist and lifted it to take a swing. "Tyler—stop!"

Before he could take action, Kyle and Abe had his arms. "Hey dude, that's not necessary."

Tyler angrily shook them off, then looked at her with disdain. "No—you're absolutely right. It's not."

He gave Jess's shoulder another slight shove as walked back into the house. Seconds later she heard the door slam.

"Is he okay to drive?" Brooke asked, her expression anxious.

Lindsay shrugged, her stomach feeling sick inside. "I—I don't know."

The fact was, she didn't know much. Why exactly she came tonight, or why she'd had the poor sense to let Tyler come with her. Or, why she was having so many doubts about her future.

She heard Tyler gun the car engine outside and within seconds he raced down the street, tires squealing.

She turned and faced the silent group of Jess's friends who stood around staring. Humiliated, she mouthed, "I'm so sorry."

Defeated, she made her way up the few steps to the deck and headed for the door.

"Wait!" Jess chased after her. "Where are you going?"

"Home. I'll call a cab." She moved for the front door, biting at her nails and wishing she'd never had the nerve to show up here tonight. She should have stayed at the DeLucas and played the dutiful wife-to-be no matter what turmoil she was experiencing.

Her mother was right—she was flighty and not centered on what mattered.

At that thought, her insides cringed. No doubt her mama would have a lot to say once she learned what had transpired tonight.

"Lindsay, let me get my keys. I'll drive you."

She nodded. "I'll wait outside.

Within minutes, Jess joined her on the front porch. He bent and picked up her knit scarf that had fallen and draped it over her shoulders, no doubt seeing the tears that had formed.

"Wanna talk about it?" he asked.

She looked over at him, not bothering to hide her miserable state. "I'm so sorry, Jess. And I'm embarrassed. I've never seen Tyler act like that."

"Can I ask you something? Why are you even with that dude? I mean, that was a complete cow plop back there." He froze, as if wanting to take the words back. "Sorry, I—"

"It's okay," she assured him. "I know what you mean. Truth is, I'm wrestling with a lot of doubt lately."

There, she'd admitted it out loud. Even so, clarity did not follow. If fact, she felt more confused than ever.

"Tyler grew up wearing the clothes that someone else laid out on the bed for him, trendy OshGosh b'Kosh when most toddlers in America were in plain Carters, know what I mean? That does something to a person. He still wears blue jeans distressed to the tune of over six hundred dollars—a metaphor for his life, I suppose." She shook her head fiercely. "The trouble is, I don't want my own children growing up being forced into designer duds. I want them to wear whatever they feel good in and not worry about what things cost."

Jess looked confused. "I kinda thought you both were—?"

"Wealthy?" Her voice grew serious and steady. "My mother would like everyone to think so," she confessed. "The truth is my father, Oscar Griffin, was a congressman. He passed away from pancreatic cancer when I was in junior high. He left us comfortable, but wealthy? No. Especially after all the medical bills rolled in."

"I'm so sorry to hear you lost your dad so early. That you had to go through all that."

Lindsay wrapped her arms around her shoulders to ward off the chill. "Thanks, Jess. It was pretty awful at the time. I still miss him every day."

Jess draped his arm across her shoulders for added warmth. "There, better?"

She nodded.

"Tell me about him."

Her eyebrows lifted. "My dad?"

He caught her eyes, held them. "Uh huh. What was he like?"

She let a tiny smile sprout at the corners of her lips. "We were really close." She let out a tiny laugh. "He always told me I was far too serious."

. "Yeah, where's the fun in that?" Jess smiled at her, that warm smile that had so drawn her to him in the first place.

Maybe that was what pulled at her again, caused her to venture sharing something she'd never told anyone else—not even her mother. "He died on a Tuesday night at seven seventeen in the evening. He was home then—under hospice care. Mom was exhausted, had gone out to get him a chocolate milk shake, his favorite. She hoped to get something down him, anything. He hadn't eaten in days. I suspect she knew from what the hospice people had told us that not eating was a sign he was nearing the end and she was desperate not to let things progress."

She took a deep breath and continued. "Anyway, I think the hospice nurse knew it too. She was attentive to his care, but I look back now and realize she was giving us more and more time alone with him. Especially because he was sleeping at longer intervals and was rarely fully awake."

Lindsay glanced upward, appreciating again the thousands of brilliant stars in the sky.

"It was me with him that night, at the very end. But before he went, he woke and we had an amazing few minutes. He feebly squeezed my hand, told me he loved me and whispered his final words through dry, cracked lips. *"No regrets."*

She felt Jess squeeze her shoulder and they both stood on the front porch gazing into the sky, neither of them saying anything for several seconds.

Jess finally broke the silence. "Seems to me he wanted you to be happy."

She sniffed, nodded. "Yes."

He turned to her. His fingers went to her cheek, the tips lightly brushing against her skin, still wet from her earlier tears. His face drew closer. She could feel his breath, smell his cologne.

She lifted her face, her eyes spanning his. She raised her hand, intending to brush away a lock of hair that had fallen onto this forehead. In doing so, the glint of the diamond on her hand caused her to flinch. She stepped back.

He pulled away as well. "So, you ready then? I'll drive you home." He plunged his hands in his pockets.

She swallowed. "Or—maybe Brooke would take me home."

He quickly nodded. "Yeah, good idea. I'll go ask her." He turned for the door, paused. "Lindsay?"

"Yeah?"

"Live is worth living with no regrets."

CHAPTER NINE

Lindsay woke from a fitful sleep to the sound of her mother talking on her phone in the other room of their suite.

"Oh Sheryl, everything was so nice last night. I'm going to have to get that bisque recipe for my own cook."

Lindsay groaned inside. Her mother was out of control. They didn't have a cook and the last she recalled, her mother didn't care for cream-based soups.

Her mother laughed. "Yes, Lindsay got in late too. No doubt they'll both need naps before the big party tonight. No, no . . . we still plan on the spa date."

She'd need a nap? What was she, a two-year-old?

Okay, yes. She was not in the best of moods. She'd wrestled on all night with the notion she'd almost kissed Jess Barnett. While she was *engaged*.

If you love someone and plan to be their wife, you don't want to kiss someone else.

Jess was a cute guy, but it wasn't even about that. There was something else about him. She'd never shared that private moment with her father with anyone, let alone a guy she hadn't known very long. Jess was easy to talk to. He had a deep soul and seemed to truly understand her.

When she was with Jess, she was a different person—a butterfly emerging from a chrysalis, no longer shackled with obligation and expectation.

Tyler, on the other hand, had been a real jerk! First, he'd acted like a fool with that blonde. When confronted, he got defensive and rude. Like a scene plucked from a bad movie, he'd played some tough guy who wrongly thought he could fix a tense situation with his fist.

She groaned.

In less than twelve hours, they would have to appear at their engagement party. Act like nothing had happened. Before she could sort through what that would mean, there was a knock at the hotel door.

Lindsay scrambled from the bed and wrapped herself in the plush hotel robe. "Mom—did you order room service?"

Her mother called to her from the other room. "No."

Lindsay tied the belt tightly around her waist and pulled her long hair into a ponytail at the back of her neck. She heard her mother open the door.

"Good morning, Tyler. What are you doing here so early? Is that a breakfast tray?"

"Morning, Julia. I need to talk to your daughter. Alone."

Lindsay could almost see her mother smile. "Well, of course. I'll head down to breakfast and leave you two lovebirds to enjoy some time." Her mother peeked her head through the open door leading to Lindsay's bed. "Honey, Tyler's here," she said in a sing-song voice. "I'm leaving, but don't forget our spa appointment this afternoon." She wiggled her fingers goodbye and pranced through the sitting area and to the door.

"Mmnn—smells good. You are so thoughtful, Tyler." She called back to Lindsay, "You snagged a good man, sweet thing."

The door closed.

Gathering her nerve, Lindsay slowly ventured out to greet her fiancé. They had a lot to talk through.

"Hey," he said, a little too brightly. He lifted the plate cover. "Ta-da!"

When she failed to react, he explained, "I had the kitchen make the pancakes in the shape of hearts. Do you like them?"

She chewed at her lip. He must feel repentant because the sentimental gesture was far out of his character.

He reached for her hand. "Look, I was a royal butt last night, and I'm sorry."

"I'm not going to argue with that."

"So, let me make it up to you." He reached into his back pocket and pulled out a light blue box—signature Tiffany. "I was going to give this to you tonight, but—"

Here's where she had a choice. Yes, he'd been a royal jerk. What good did it do to rub his nose in the fact? The only viable solution was to confront the underlying factors with open honesty. She owed him at least that.

"Thank you, Tyler." She leaned and kissed his cheek. He smelled good, like he'd just stepped from the shower. "That was really thoughtful," she said, taking the box from his hand.

"Well, open it," he urged.

She sunk into a chair. Her fingers worked the tiny ribbon until it fell loose from the box. Before lifting the lid, she grinned up at him.

Inside was a stunning diamond tennis bracelet.

"Oh, Tyler. It's really beautiful." She lifted the delicate piece of jewelry and handed it to him.

He fastened it on her wrist. "So, you like it?"

She lifted it to the light. "Yes, I do. Very much."

No doubt the gesture was a great start, but she needed to tell him how she was feeling.

"Tyler, I'm having a hard time with all this."

"This?"

She motioned for him to sit. Instead, he snared hold of the belt on her bathroom, gave it a tug.

"We're alone," he said suggestively. "All alone."

Lindsay slapped his hand away. "Tyler, I'm trying to talk to you."

Resigned, he stepped back. He held up his palms and sunk into the seat opposite her. "Okay, okay—I get it. I'm listening."

Now that she had his attention, she didn't even know how to communicate how she'd been feeling. She took a deep breath. "Ty—this whole wedding thing is getting out of hand. I mean, our mothers have taken over and put us on stage like some circus monkeys. Your dad is pulling your puppet strings. You've become a marionette responding to his every move. These people, they—well, I can hardly relate to most of them."

Tyler reached for her. "What are you saying?"

"I'm saying, we're not even *us* anymore." She leaned forward. "All of this is making me crazy. Add to that what happened last night. I mean, I'm not even sure—"

She thought she saw fear in his eyes.

"Are you calling off the engagement?"

Was she?

No, she wasn't ready for a step that big and she told him so. "Look, Tyler—tonight we're going to celebrate our decision to spend our lives together at a wonderful party with a lot of people. I think it's important that we don't gloss over what lead to our tiff last night."

He slipped in next to her, put his arm around her shoulder. "Okay, shoot. What do you want me to know?"

Lindsay took a deep breath, appreciating that he was willing to listen. "I don't want to wake up ten years from now and see all my dreams behind me. I don't want my children raised by nannies. I don't want to schedule time with you between travel itineraries."

Her looked at her incredulously, pulled his arm back. "That's what this was all about? The reason you snuck off and went skiing? Why you wanted to attend that ridiculous party?"

He no doubt saw her reaction and waved his hands to stop her response. "No, I'm sorry. I shouldn't have said that. But you'd have to admit, Lindsay—you've been acting really strange lately. I mean, I thought you were excited about our engagement and all this."

"Oh, I am," she quickly assured him. "Well, maybe not everything our mothers have—"

"Taken over?"

She couldn't contain her smile. "I wasn't going to say it like that."

Tyler wove his fingers through her own. "I just need for you not to run from me. This life we're about to embark on might present some bumps along the way, but we're in that one percent you hear mentioned on all the television news shows—the indubitable group of people known as the lucky ones. We'll get to enjoy things the masses won't, and so will our children."

Lindsay studied his face. "Just assure me that our children will also enjoy the gift of our being present, that they'll get *us*. I want them to have a normal life, with normal parents. I want that for me."

"Okay, I get it." He reached and took her hands. "Let's just try and get through this weekend and then I'll talk to my parents. I warn you, there are obligations that come with becoming a DeLuca. I told you that. But, I'll ask my parents to tone it down a bit. You can talk with your mom and we'll go on from there. Sound like a plan?"

She let out the breath she didn't even realize she'd been holding. "Yes, that sounds like a good start. And, I want something else." She paused. "I want your time. We have several hours before the party and I want to take you up on Bald Mountain, show you the view. Maybe we can have lunch. Just the two of us."

He hesitated. "I think Dad—" He stopped, recognized this was a test. "No, I'll make that happen. We're expecting a call on a very important deal we're putting together, a public offering . . . but yeah, I can do that."

"Oh no." Lindsay's hopes deflated. "I forgot I have to go to the spa with your mother."

Tyler held up his forefinger. He slid his iPhone from his pocket and worked his thumb across the tiny screen. "Done," he said. "I texted both our mothers—told them I was kidnapping my bride-to-be for the day and I didn't want any argument."

Lindsay raised her eyebrows. "You can do

that?"

He bent and kissed her forehead. "For you, Lindsay? Anything."

* * *

Her first clue the trip up the mountain wasn't going to go as planned was when Tyler pressed what looked like a wad of bills into the attendant's hand upon loading. Second clue, when no one else got in the passenger lift with them, despite the long line at the gondola booth.

"What's going on?" she asked as doors closed and the overhead engine started to grind and whirr. The car they were riding in lifted and swung slightly before settling into a steady pace forward.

Tyler arched his eyebrow at her and formed a naughty grin, looking like a kid in junior high who'd been caught with his brother's magazine— the one hidden under the bed.

"Oh, get serious!" she told him as he started to unzip his coat. "You're kidding, right?"

"Not sure who had the idea for you to play

roomies with your mother this weekend, but that entire plan stinks." He moved forward, his fingers unzipping her coat.

Lindsay scooted back from him. "Tyler, I mean it. We are not going to do what you have in mind—not in a gondola with windows."

Her protests didn't phase him. "Who's going to see us up here?" He pressed against her, captured her mouth with his.

Shallow breaths rose from her throat at the warmth of his skin, the insistence in his voice. Still, this was ridiculous. They couldn't get intimate now—not up here!

"Tyler, stop. I mean it." She stifled a giggle and pushed him back. "The entire lift ride will be over. We'll be at the top and in no position to be seen. Are you hearing me?"

"Oh, you're no fun. Besides, who said we have to remove our clothes? We can simply get creative and—"

That's when the next clue came. Tyler's phone rang.

He sighed and pulled the phone from his pants pocket, then held up a finger. "I need to get this."

Her gaze cut to the snowy vista outside the gondola, hoping their earlier conversation helped him to understand the things she'd been wrestling in her mind as of late.

"Now?" she heard him say. "Well, yeah Dad. I understand. Yes, I get it. Sure. Look just conference me in. Where am I?" Tyler looked over at her. "I'll explain later. But no problem. I'll take the call."

He hung up, stress written all over his face.

"Everything okay?" she asked.

He assured her everything was fine. "I'm sorry, but I am going to have to take a call when it comes in. But, I'll make it up to you," he told her.

Her hand drifted to his knee. "It's all right. Really. I understand." Lindsay wasn't naïve. Of course there would be times he'd have to put the business above all else. Her concern was that she needed to know his general philosophy matched her own. If that were so, they could work out the day-to-day decisions and remain in unison as they started their new life together.

She wanted to say so but Tyler's phone rang

again.

He answered. "Hello?"

His brows drew together. "Hello?" he repeated.

He pulled the phone from his ear, glanced around. "Damn, the reception just went." With the phone back at his ear, he tried again. "Hello?"

Tyler banged the phone against his leg, as if that would help clear the problem.

"What's the matter?" Lindsay asked.

He ignored her. In a near panic, he punched the screen with his forefinger. "Nothing," he said in a near growl. "What the hell did you force me up here for anyway? Of course, there's no cell service on this stupid mountain."

"Honey, calm down—"

"Don't tell me to calm down!" he shouted. "You have no idea how critical it is that I take this call. You think everything is just *join hands and hearts kumbaya*? Well, it's not."

He tried again. When the necessary reception failed, he slammed the phone against the wall of the gondola, sending a tiny piece of plastic flying past her head. "This is why I don't do this crap."

"I don't think breaking the phone is going to help."

"See, that's the problem." He glared at her. "I don't need you to think."

He might as well have slapped her across the face. "I see."

Tyler closed his eyes against the weight of what had escaped his mouth. "Lindsay, don't. You know I didn't mean that." He reached for her. "I love you."

Lindsay pulled back, glared at him in disgust. "Now who's getting all *kumbaya*?"

"Baby, please."

Her sigh was ragged and full of pain. The realization of what he'd let slip from his mouth in anger penetrated all the way to her heart, which sat in her chest like a heavy lump of ice. "Tyler, just stop." Weighing her next words, she quietly added, "We both know you just broke more than your phone."

With a gasp, Tyler grabbed her arm. "Geez, Lindsay! I'm sorry. Come on. Don't do this. Our party is in less than six hours," he reminded her, pleading.

She gently pulled her arm free.

With a sick feeling in the pit of her stomach, it dawned on her that she was in an impossible situation. No matter what he'd said, she wasn't the sort to create a public spectacle.

"I'm not calling off the engagement party, if that's what you're worried about," she told him with a hint of frost in her voice.

Relief spread. "Oh, thank God. I was afraid—" He paused, examining her with his eyes, questioning. "So, we're okay then?" he asked, hopeful.

Lindsay turned and looked out at the clouds rolling in over the mountains in the distance, the way they hid the snow-topped peaks and made the horizon look less sharp.

"Let's just get through the party," she finally managed, her voice catching.

After that, she knew there were no guarantees.

CHAPTER TEN

Some things couldn't easily be forgotten, no matter how hard you tried. Even so, Lindsay knew how important this engagement party was to both their mothers. She was determined to play her part—even if a decision she never wanted to make weighed heavy on her heart. A decision that would alter all their lives in one way or another. Most of all, her own.

In what seemed like the blink of an eye, the reality curtains got pulled back and Tyler's true character was revealed, his volatile nature when he was under pressure.

Pretty words were just that. They could never erase the ugliness of what he'd been conditioned to believe—or his lack of respect for her.

She just needed to get through tonight.

Starting at five o'clock, beautifully dressed guests were shuttled to the Trail Creek Cabin in a horse drawn sleigh for signature cocktails cleverly named *Mint to be Berried*—a concoction of lemon vodka and mottled berries served in martini glasses garnished with fresh mint.

At six-thirty, everyone moved to the pavilion for dinner, normally available only in summer, but with special accommodations now housed hundreds of well-wishers in warmth and style.

Despite the conflict she carried inside, Lindsay was swept up in the storybook event as Tyler grabbed her hand and they made their grand entrance.

The crowd erupted with applause.

Tyler beamed and held up his palms. "Thank you, everyone. Thank you." His hand went to her back as he took an offered microphone. "Lindsay and I both appreciate all of you taking time out of your busy lives to gather here in Sun Valley, Idaho to celebrate this special event with us." He looked around the venue, nodded to several people he recognized, then turned his attention on her. "Can you believe this beautiful woman agreed to marry a chump like me?"

Delighted chuckles broke out across the pavilion.

"And one more thing," he added. "I want to express gratitude to my parents, Charles and Sheryl DeLuca and to Lindsay's mother, Julia Griffin, for all your support and for this amazing party."

He pointed to her mother. "As you know, Julia—your daughter is far too difficult to impress, but I think even she would have to agree this celebration is over-the-top."

Lindsay smiled and leaned into the microphone. "Yes, everything is so beautiful. Thank you."

They mingled. She met so many people, she could barely keep the names straight. She was reintroduced to Jonathan and Dottie Stewart, lifelong friends of the DeLucas and to Mr. and Mrs. Michaels, the potential clients Tyler had met with earlier in the day.

"That dress is gorgeous, dear. Who's the designer?" Mrs. Michaels asked.

Before she could respond, her mother appeared by her side, handed off her empty martini glass to a server. "It's a Carolina Herrera. Lindsay and I have always been in love with her classic lines."

That spawned a discussion about rack buys versus custom—a conversation that droned on until dinner was announced.

They sat at tables covered in creamy linens and table settings one might see in the pages of a magazine. Crystal chandeliers hung from the upper crossbars and fresh bouquets of peach-colored tea roses served as centerpieces. A live orchestra played on a raised stage at one end of the pavilion where the dance floor awaited.

Dinner consisted of roasted leg of lamb served with potato hash, a goat cheese walnut soufflé with watercress and frisee salad served by white-gloved wait staff.

Lindsay tucked a pressed napkin across her lap, prepared herself for a long and tedious discussion she prayed wouldn't turn to wedding plans. She was doing well to get through this party without trying to fake excitement over a ceremony she wasn't sure would take place.

Who changes her mind about marrying someone while sitting at her engagement party?

The irony of the situation left her heart aching. She'd never contemplated she might retract her decision to become Tyler's wife when she'd stepped into the beautiful lobby of the Sun Valley Lodge only a couple of days ago.

Tyler, of course, would be humiliated. His parents furious. And her own mother? She shuddered thinking about how she'd single-handedly be pulling the rug out from under her mama. Ruining dreams the woman had described at length throughout her growing up years, more markedly after her daddy died.

Doubt gathered in the pit of her stomach when she considered the impact.

"Ma'am, sparkling water or plain?"

She looked up, startled to see a familiar face grinning at her. "Jess?"

"Hey, Lindsay." He held up a pitcher in one hand and a blue labeled bottle in the other.

She didn't bother to hide her delight as she pointed to the bottle. "Why didn't you mention you were working our party?"

"The resort ended up short-staffed tonight." He pointed the neck of the bottle at her goblet and poured. "I offered to help Karyn out and fill in."

Jess nodded in Tyler's direction. "Hey, Tyler. Good to see you again."

Tyler, who had remained quiet up until now, took a deep sip of his wine and barely nodded back. He held his stemmed goblet and swirled the cabernet in a slow circle. "The legs on this vintage are remarkable. Could we get another bottle here at the table?"

She hated his dismissive tone. The way he seemed to relish the fact Jess was serving their table was the one of the very reasons she had to reconsider her future.

Jess, on the other hand, was cordial. Even after the nastiness of last night. "Sure thing, Tyler," he responded.

Tyler's dad broke free from a discussion with Mr. Paulson, an oilman from Houston, and focused his attention on Jess. "You know each other?"

Lindsay placed her fingertips on the arm of

Tyler's suit jacket. "I'm sorry. How rude of me—yes, everyone, this is Jess Barnett. He's a new friend."

"Oh?" She detected an edge to her future father-in-law's voice.

"We met over in the lodge," Jess quickly told him. "I noticed Lindsay checking out the celebrity photos in the hallway and introduced myself."

Her mother fingered her pearls, gave Jess a sidelong look. "How nice." Lindsay could guess her mother thought the situation was anything but. She hid it well. "We've found the entire staff to be so helpful. Everything about the resort is top quality. I can see why so many celebrities chose Sun Valley as their vacation destination, both then and now."

"Jess took me skiing," Lindsay blurted, a little louder than she'd intended.

Every head at their table suddenly turned.

Under the table, Tyler's hand went to her leg and applied pressure in a silent message, but she didn't let that stop her. "Jess and his friends were kind enough to invite me to share a few runs on Baldy yesterday morning. I had a fabulous time."

The look on her mother's face was one of pure horror.

Tyler took another sip. He slowly smiled and turned to Jess. "Yes, that was so nice of you to take our girl up the mountain and show her a good time." He looked directly at Lindsay. "In fact, where are my manners. Please, won't you join us?" He stood and waved over another staff member. "Can you get an extra chair at this table please."

Jess immediately turned flustered. "Oh, I can't. I'm working."

Tyler waved him off. "Nonsense. We're paying for this shindig and want you as our guest. Your bosses can't argue with that. You've been very generous with your hospitality this weekend and I simply want to reciprocate."

Lindsay began to regret her brazen approach to challenging her fiancé's bias. "Tyler, honey—I don't think that's a good idea."

Tyler tossed back his head and laughed. "Babe, of course it's a good idea. Jess here is a friend and I want him to celebrate with us." He looked to Jess. "So, sit down." To the server, he added, "Bring this guy a plate, will you?"

Jess looked like a trapped animal. He complied, tossing an apologetic look Lindsay's way.

Tyler's mother looked confused. Even so, she instantly turned the gracious hostess. "Jess, please sit. We're so happy to have you with us."

Lindsay was grateful, and gave her a brief look that said so.

She'd been a fool to feed the tension, especially given what had happened last night and in the gondola today. For good measure, she reached for Tyler's hand and gave it a squeeze.

He smiled back at her. A good sign.

Her mother waited for Jess to be served. "So, where exactly do you live, Mr. Barnett? Here in Sun Valley?"

Jess let out a chuckle. "Goodness, no. Prices are far too steep. My friends and I rent a place in Bellevue, a tiny community south of here." He paused. "Well, at least for part of the year. After the winter season, it's all up in the air."

She could almost see her mother's nose twitch. "Oh, I see," she said.

Tyler pulled his hand from her own. He lifted

124

his empty glass to the server while never taking his eyes from Jess, watching as he explained.

"It's like this, ma'am—I kind of work my way from place to place."

Her mom lifted her eyebrows, placed her hand against her chest. "Goodness, you find that lifestyle appealing?"

Jess smoothed his hair and shrugged. "Well, yes—I do. I've got everything I need. Air in my lungs, good friends. I love waking up every morning not knowing exactly what's going to happen." He paused, looked at Lindsay. "Or, who I'm going to meet."

Her friend lifted his water goblet to the server and waited for it to be filled. "You see, I believe life's a gift and I don't intend to waste a minute of it—or look over my shoulder with regret." He looked pointedly in Lindsay's direction and shrugged. "I think that's a pretty good plan."

She caught his message and granted him a timid smile.

Mrs. DeLuca looked at him full-on with appreciation. "Well said, Mr. Barnett."

"Please, call me Jess."

Tyler chimed in. "Sounds a little freestyle to those of us who shoulder responsibility."

Jess grinned back at him. "Ah, maybe. I suppose a person needs to own who they are."

Lindsay resisted the urge to giggle. She'd never seen anyone confident enough to stand up to Tyler. Even if with sublime subtlety.

The expression on her mama's face was not so subtle. "I have to agree with Tyler. Didn't someone famous say the price of greatness is responsibility?"

A tiny pulse beat in Mr. DeLuca's set jaw. "Winston Churchill." September 6, 1943 at an address he presented at Harvard University."

Her mama pointed a well-manicured nail into the air. "Yes. Winston Churchill."

When they'd finished their entrees, Tyler tossed his napkin onto the table and traded in his wine glass for a snifter of fine brandy, mentioning twice how this particular Armagnac was extremely rare. "The subtle notes caramel and toffee notes are due to a special distilling process as the grapes ferment and age. Like fine wine, the character comes from the wood in the oak barrels." He turned to Jess. "Mr. Barnett, you aren't having a glass?"

Her friend held up his palms. "Oh, none for me thanks. I'm more a beer kind of guy."

Lindsay stifled a chuckle.

Tyler caught her reaction. His brooding demeanor turned dark. "Are you sure? Not often a server gets to sample a fine liquor that costs more than his night's wages."

The comment sucked the air from the table. From his expression, even his father seemed to believe his son was being rude.

Lindsay wanted to blame her fiancé's behavior on the alcohol he'd been heavily drinking. Truth was, not even that could excuse the way he'd taken every chance to pull Jess down and step on him. An ugly repeat of the night before.

She glared at Tyler, studied her fiancé more carefully, as a woman does when the man she was to marry turns into an egocentric monster before her very eyes. His arrogance was appalling and moved her to acknowledge what she'd been reluctant to admit.

She no longer was sure she wanted to be

Mrs. Tyler DeLuca.

* * *

After what seemed like an interminable length of time, dessert was finally served and the dance floor was made ready.

Jess rose from the table. "Well, folks . . . I appreciate the time with you all, but I need to excuse myself and get back to my duties." He turned specifically to Lindsay's mother. "Thank you for your hospitality."

"Certainly," her mother said, extending her hand to shake his. "It was nice meeting you, Mr. Barnett."

When he'd gone, Tyler adjusted the lapels of his dinner jacket. "I guess it's time for me to dance with my lovely bride-to-be." He gave Lindsay a wide smile, but she couldn't quite make herself smile back as she accepted his hand and dutifully followed him to the dance floor.

"Was all that really necessary?" she whispered angrily as he leaned into her. She pasted a smile as they began to sway to the music, aware everyone in the room was watching.

"What are you talking about? I was trying to be cordial."

So, that's how he was going to play this.

She'd always found passive-aggressive behavior unattractive. In fact, there was a lot of things she was discovering about Tyler that niggled at her, made her second guess her decision to marry him.

She looked around the room at the smiling faces. In a few minutes the toasts would begin, with their closest of family and friends lavishing good wishes on the perfect couple.

But they weren't the perfect couple.

Slowly but surely, she and Tyler were quickly drifting apart. The marriage she'd wanted was no more. As for this new future, she couldn't say where it was going or even if they'd be on the journey together.

She couldn't very well move forward now that she believed Tyler was the wrong man for her. Why hadn't she seen that before?

Her mother sat at the table reveling in the knowledge her daughter was going to marry into the DeLuca family. No doubt, she'd be heartbroken to learn her daughter was having such severe doubts about the upcoming wedding. The disappointment would be devastating.

Tyler's thumb gently moved against her back. He hummed in her ear.

Even though he'd revealed a side she didn't care for, she was grateful to have learned that they were incompatible now, before she committed to spend her entire life with him. No doubt, he'd take her breaking off their engagement hard. He and his parents would be angry after throwing this big public party and having to pull back from all the big wedding plans. These kinds of humiliations just didn't happen in their social circle.

Just the thought of it made her feel a bit clammy and breathless.

She struggled to take in a deep breath. Through the fog of building nerves, she recognized the orchestra had started a new song, a sentimental favorite of her daddy's—*Let's Stay Together* by Al Green.

Oh, goodness.

Her pulse beat faster. She fought to gain control as several couples made their way to the dance floor. Out of the corner of her eye, she saw his parents stand. Charles took Sheryl's hand and led her out to join them.

Lindsay's hands went clammy, her ears rang a little.

Tyler pulled back and looked at her. "Are you all right?"

She shook her head no. "I—I think I need some air."

Tyler scowled. "Are you kidding?" he whispered. "Now?"

She nodded, now embarrassed. "I—I'm okay." Remarkably, she kept her face calm, even though her heart was now pounding so hard she thought it might dance off without her.

He pasted a smile and pulled her tighter. "I don't know what's going on inside that head of yours, but I love you. You know that, don't you?"

She nodded again. "I do know that." She forced a brilliant smile. "Hey, maybe this is a good time for you to dance with my mom," she suggested, anxious to stave off the panic attack she was fighting. All she needed was to get outside, alone.

"Yeah, okay." He led her off the dance floor and back to their table. "Mrs. Griffin, may I have the pleasure?"

Her mama stood, bathed in the glow of the moment.

Lindsay took the opportunity to make her escape. She headed for the back door.

Outside, the air was cool and the stars overhead bright.

She wrapped her arms around her shoulders, relishing the chill. Almost immediately, her panic symptoms receded.

"Hey, there." Jess appeared out of nowhere. "What's wrong? You okay?"

She nodded, unbidden tears forming. "I—I couldn't—breathe in there."

Jess removed his jacket, wrapped it around her shoulders. "Here, just close your eyes. Think of good things. Sunshine overhead and powder beneath your feet." His voice was soothing.

She found herself wishing she didn't have to go back inside, that instead she could just stare into the star-filled night and listen to his voice.

"I—I think I'm making a mistake," she told him.

"Then don't marry him."

"But—"

"Don't marry him, Lindsay."

"What's going on out here?" Her mother's voice was like a rock breaking through glass. "Lindsay, what's going on?"

Lindsay tried to form a cogent appeal as she stepped forward. "I didn't feel very well," she muttered.

From the razor look in her eyes, her mother wasn't buying it.

Lindsay glanced over her shoulder. Her gaze fell on Jess who was standing watching them.

"Uh, if you could excuse me—I need to get back to my duties," he said as he brushed past them and headed for the door.

She hadn't known prior to the moment their eyes met on his way past her that your world could sometimes be found in another person's face. He understood things that the others couldn't, simply because he took the time to observe.

Lindsay swallowed hard, battling something bubbling up within her that she couldn't seem to force down. It was terrifying—she wasn't ready—but there was no stopping what dared came out of her mouth.

"I know you're not ready to hear this, Mama . . . I love you. I really do—but I'm having doubts. About Tyler."

"Nonsense." Her mother grabbed her arm, whispered angrily, "I don't know what you are doing, young lady, but it stops now. This is not some game where you pass go and get another chance. Do you understand?"

Lindsay's eyes grew wide. She was shaken, already knowing she'd made a mistake in opening up to her mama. She'd been stupid to blurt out her feelings in the manner she had. The honesty was crippling.

Her mother didn't bother to hide how tightly she was controlling her own emotions. She simply moved her daughter toward the door. "Come inside. Everyone's waiting."

Lindsay pulled back slightly. "Calm down, Mama," she said, firmly. "I'm not going to make a scene tonight if that's what you're worried about. Nothing has been decided. But, we do need to talk . . . about a lot of things."

CHAPTER ELEVEN

Julia Griffin ripped the earrings from her lobes and tossed them on the bedside table. "You are not to see that boy again—understand?"

Lindsay's jaw tightened. While she loved her mother, she was no longer a little girl who could be ordered to obey. She moved for the bathroom, determined not to respond.

"Excuse me, young lady. This is far too important to walk away from."

Lindsay felt her patience running thin. "It's best if we leave this discussion alone for now, Mama. We've had a big night, it's very late. Let's just go to bed." She again turned for the bathroom, her insides churning.

Her mother grabbed her arm and whirled her

around. "Lindsay, I forbid you to pursue any level of friendship with this Jess character. It's nothing but foolishness, especially under the circumstances. In case you've forgotten, you are about to become Mrs. Tyler DeLuca."

She rolled her eyes, now angry. "Oh stop it Mama. It's not at all what you are imagining. This isn't about Jess. And I did not invite him to sit at our table. Tyler did."

Her mother's hackles visibly rose. "Do not get smart with me." She paced the room, hands on her hips. "Our situation is precarious. You know money is very limited."

"Of course I know. You remind me often." She stiffened, determined to hold her ground. "Daddy's earning income was hampered by his choices. As a government servant, he failed to build the kind of estate that would ensure our place in society after he was gone. And I am very lucky to have this card to play—to become a member of the DeLuca family. A move that would change our lot in life." She fought back a light laugh. "Did I miss anything?"

Her mother huffed. "I don't understand you,

Lindsay. This match isn't only about social stand-ing—you marrying well ensures our financial sur-vival."

Lindsay grew furious. "How can you put that on my shoulders?"

Her mother glared back. "Why are you being so selfish?"

"I—I'm being selfish?" Her open hand pounded at her chest. "This is my life, Mama. Do you get that? It's the only one I have. Who I spend it with is my decision—and only mine." She couldn't remember ever raising her voice to her mother, but she was too angry to censor her emo-tions. "Lately, I've noticed things that worry me. Tyler's rapidly morphing into someone I don't even know. His actions tonight reveal a warped sense of entitlement I'm not sure I want to be part of for the next forty plus years."

Her mother's eyes sprouted tears. "Don't say that! Do you want me to have to get some job? Maybe as a greeter at Walmart? That's all I'm trained for," she said, her voice choked. "Is that what you want?"

Lindsay sighed. "Don't be so dramatic. You

have Grandma's trust."

Her mother rubbed at her forehead. She took a deep breath. "Oh, baby. You don't get it. How do you think I paid for your schooling? Your car?" She flung her arms wide. "This party and the upcoming wedding deposits. Where do you think my ability to pay for all that came from?"

Lindsay swallowed against her tightening throat. "What are you saying?"

Her mother picked up on Lindsay's softening and went in for the kill. "With no way to replenish our finances, to get back on top of all this, I'll go down."

Lindsay sunk to the sofa and vehemently shook her head. "I would never let that happen. I can work, you know."

"What about our house?" Her mother continued to pace. "Do you have any idea the amount it takes to keep up a place like that? Property that is on the historical register and has been in your father's family for years?" She dragged her hand through her hair. "What about your daddy's reputation? What will people say if they learn he died and left his wife and daughter without any financial means?"

Her mother slid to the sofa and grabbed Lindsay's hands. "Tyler loves you. You love him. I don't understand the problem."

Lindsay looked away—closed her eyes. "I just want to be happy, Mama."

Her mother took her chin and raised her face to her own. "Listen to me, baby girl. A lifestyle like that Barnett boy embraces might sound glamorous, but it's not. That carefree mode wears very thin after a while, when there's no money to travel, to buy nice things, to lavish gifts on your children with unfettered restraint. Look down the road at a life with Tyler—to what that means."

"Choose carefully." She rose. "Your future and that of your children depends on what you decide." Her mother paused, wiped the wet from her cheek. "Life doesn't come with a rewind button."

* * *

Brooke and Abe sat on the sofa, a big bowl with only a few popcorn kernels left at the bottom wedged between them. An old Seinfeld episode played on the television mounted on the wall, which had been muted.

"Are you kidding me?" Brooke asked, her eyes wide. "I can't believe that Tyler guy actually said that? In front of everyone?"

Abe nodded his head in agreement. "I agree, dude. That's pretty messed up."

Jess ran his hand through his hair. "Yeah, I wasn't sure how to—well, I mean, the guy's a class A jerk. Still, maybe I should have just—"

"Oh, please," Brooke interrupted. "What occurred at that table was not on your shoulders. Lindsay's fiancé has horrible manners. I can't believe he acted like that."

Abe shrugged. "Jealousy can make us guys do some stupid things."

Jess scowled. "Jealousy?"

A grin sprouted on his buddy's face. "Yeah. Think about it. His very pretty fiancé skips out on all the party happenings and goes skiing with some dude she'd just met. Someone he didn't even know. Rattled him up a bit. It happens."

"Guess I hadn't considered that" Jess admitted.

"Still, it doesn't excuse what he said. He was extremely rude—to you, and by extension to Lindsay." Brooke took a deep breath. "And that scene here at the house the other night? Truth is, I can't believe she's engaged to that guy." She turned to Abe, grabbed his hand. "If you ever treated me like that, it'd be over."

Abe moved the bowl and draped his arm around Brooke's shoulder. "So noted."

"Do you think she loves him?" Brooke asked.

Jess stared at them. "She's engaged to marry Tyler. Of course she loves him."

"Are you sure? Because I see the way she looks at you."

Now they were just talking nonsense. "I don't know what you're suggesting, but you're wrong," he told them, passing his hand over the back of his neck.

Brooke shook her head. "Do you forget that I drove her home after that party? I personally think she's having a lot of doubt and believes she's with the wrong guy, which only became apparent to her after she met you."

"Don't hang any of this on me. I'm not the sort to get in the way of—"

"Of what?" she challenged. "Falling in love?"

Abe exchanged glances with Brooke. "Yeah, you should see your face when you're around her. You should tell her how you feel, don't you think?"

Their comments made him feel stormy inside. He'd never meddle with someone else's relationship. Even if he wanted to. The only motive he had in the situation was to support Lindsay in whatever decision she made.

At least that's what he told himself when he fell into bed later than night and couldn't get her out of his mind.

CHAPTER TWELVE

After a fitful sleep, Lindsay woke to an unusually quiet hotel suite. Outside the window, an overnight drop in temperature left Baldy Mountain cloaked in low-hanging clouds, the sky gray and thick with impending snow.

"Mama," she called out. "You here?"

Meeting with silence, she swung the thick duvet cover aside and climbed from the bed, dread building as she remembered their tense exchange, and all that faced her now.

She pulled her chilled arms through the sleeves of her robe and wandered to the bathroom, stopping to place a log on the smoldering fireplace. The bathroom tiles felt like ice against her bare feet, forcing her back for her slippers.

Her mama must still be mad to have left without waking her. But then, she was mad too. She was faced with nothing but nothing but bad options. No matter which way she turned, what she decided about her future, someone she cared about would be hurt.

Unable to find her own slippers, she slipped into her mother's and made a second try for the bathroom. Leaning against the massive marble countertop, she gazed in the mirror. Her reflection showed clear signs of her rough night—circles under her eyes, matted hair and sallow skin color.

She was about to jump in the shower when she noticed the post it attached to the bathroom counter.

Lindsay – Went into Ketchum to meet Charles and Sheryl for breakfast. Our flight leaves tonight at seven. You'll want to pack. ~Mama

Her hands dove deep into her robe pockets.

Here was the thing. There was no missing the disappointment evident in that note. Disappointment that she alone had caused.

No one could argue her mama could be pushy and often failed to listen to any other point of view when she had her mind set on a certain direction. The truth was her mother would walk on water for her. There was no doubting that. Her motives were not only financially motivated, but also based on what she thought was best for her daughter.

Her mama had never missed a single concert, play, soccer game, track meet, Brownie meeting, choral performance. She packed a healthy lunch every day, including one indulgent Reese's candy bar on Fridays. She wrote encouraging notes and arrived fifteen minutes early for school pickup, so she would never have to stand in the parking lot alone.

More than once, her mama had stayed up all night helping her study for a biology exam, or a math test. She'd hated it—struggled in both subjects, but her mama wouldn't let up. "You can do it!" she claimed.

When it was time to search for colleges, Lindsay recalled their first exploratory trip with fondness, the way they giggled and planned her future. "Dream big," her mama urged. "Never stop dreaming big."

To say she felt conflicted by her decision and all that was ahead was an understatement. Even given the financial debacle her mother had created.

She wasn't necessarily a church goer, but she was going to need some divine guidance on how to maneuver this mess.

After a quick shower, Lindsay pulled on a pair of jeans and a pink sweater, pulled her hair back into a ponytail and headed for the door.

Despite the early hour, the lobby was brimming with vacationers. A cute couple posed near the fireplace for a picture, their three adorable children in matching ski sweaters.

Karyn aimed their camera and clicked off some photos. "There you go," she said, smiling.

She noticed Lindsay and waved. "Hey!" She moved in her direction. "I hear everything went marvelous last night." Karyn leaned and gave Lindsay a little hug. "I'm so very happy for you and Tyler."

"Oh, the entire party was wonderful," Lindsay said, a little too quickly. She felt tongue-tied and jumbled up. Had she really just said that? Had she meant it?

It was entirely possible Karyn might soon learn otherwise, possible Jess might spill to the contrary. That seemed out of character for him, but it was possible.

It dawned on her that at least part of her angst came from knowing her new friend had witnessed her falling apart—twice. They'd only known each other a few days, yet more than any other human being on the face of this earth, Jess Barnett was privy to just how conflicted she felt about her impending marriage to Tyler DeLuca. The knowledge felt like the tug of a wool sweater that rubbed.

"Is something wrong?" Karyn asked.

"Oh, no. Nothing's wrong." She replaced her sour expression with a manufactured bright smile. "I guess I was just thinking how much I'd like to show my appreciation to my mother and to Tyler's—a gift for all they did to pull together such an extraordinary gala."

"I know just the thing," Karyn volunteered. The hospitality director guided her to the gift shop. "I'm sure you can find the right sentiment on these shelves."

Lindsay brightened. "Yes, that's a great idea. Look at all these beautiful pieces of jewelry." She moved to a glass counter, picked up a stunning pendant in a delicate setting of gold. "What is this stone? It's gorgeous."

The shopkeeper joined them. "That's Bruneau Jasper found over in Owyhee County. I love the color striations." She lifted the reading glasses hanging on a chain around her neck and placed them on her nose. "See there," she pointed. "The way the hues sharpen on the table of the cabochon."

Lindsay beamed. "It's really beautiful."

Karyn leaned in for a better look. "Greek to me, but I know the local artisan. Her name is Trudy Dilworth—Miss Trudy to the locals. She owns a shop located in Giacobbi Square."

The lady behind the sales counter nodded. "Miss Trudy is one of the most respected jewelry makers in the field. She also paints."

"Yes, I've taken some of her classes," Karyn said. "Miss Trudy is a master of her craft."

A sharp pang of yearning formed inside

Lindsay. "I've always dreamed of creating artistry items and finding a market for them."

Karyn's face lit up. "Hey, you want to meet her?"

Lindsay gaped back at the two women. "You could arrange that?"

Her elation was short-lived. She was to have lunch with Tyler and she and her mother were scheduled to fly out this evening.

Lindsay let out a disappointed sigh. "Oh, I'd love to. Unfortunately, I'm afraid there's no time." She looked across the glass counter to the shop-keeper, crestfallen at the prospect of missing out on the opportunity. "But, I will purchase this pen-dant and those matching earrings." She turned to Karyn. "I think they'll love these items. Thank you."

Karyn's mouth curved into a wide smile. "Hopefully, you'll be back to visit us sometime. We could arrange something then."

The idea of returning to Sun Valley someday lifted her spirits. "I'd love that."

Back in the lobby, she pulled her phone from her purse intending to text her mother, tell her she was sorry. While a decision still loomed, she'd been horribly insensitive to ruin the weekend for her mama.

She placed her thumbs on the tiny screen when her phone dinged and a text from Tyler appeared.

"Babe, I hate to do this to you but Dad wants me to conference in with some investors. I'm going to have to push back our lunch. Can you meet me at a placed called Crusty's at one thirty? I'm dying for a good steak before we head home. I love you ~T"

She sighed and texted back. *"Sure. See you then. Love—"*

She swallowed and backspaced. *"See you then. ~L"*

Outside the lobby windows, a man and a woman glided across the ice, skating in perfect synchronization. Their movements were graceful and lovely—two operating as one.

Truth was, she and Tyler had fallen out of sync. More and more, she came in second behind the business. Worse, their dreams and aspirations seemed to be going in opposite directions.

No doubt she had a lot to sort out.

It also dawned on her that their postponed lunch date opened up her schedule. Maybe she could take the opportunity to drop in on that woman's art studio after all. How hard could it be to find Giacobbi Square?

Twenty minutes later, Lindsay stood at the door of a cute little shop with gabled roofline and a sign that read Painted Lady. She wasn't sure if she was supposed to knock but ended up gently pushing open the door. A little bell mounted above the door jamb tinkled.

"Oh, hello there!" A rather large woman wearing flowing red pants and a multi-colored top that looked like a native American blanket made of wool made her way across the brightly lit room with shelves lined with painting supplies. In the center were easels and empty chairs. "I'm Trudy Dilworth. And who might you be, dear?" She rubbernecked and looked out the windows. "No car? Oh, of course. You must've taken the shuttle."

Before Lindsay could respond, the woman added, "You're not from around here. A tourist?" She held up one finger. "No, don't tell me. I think

I saw your photo in the Idaho Mtn. Express. You're that gal from back east who is getting married—yes, to that handsome and very well off DeLuca boy." She winked. "A diamond catch among gems, eh?"

Lindsay took her outstretched hand. "I hope I'm not interrupting—"

"No, no—not at all." Trudy shook with enthusiasm. "Happy for the company. What can I do for you, dear?" She paused, a worried look sprouting. "I hope you're not wanting to take a class. My next one doesn't start until two this afternoon."

Lindsay shook her head. "This morning I was in the gift shop at the Sun Valley Lodge and bought some of your pieces. The hospitality director—"

"Karyn Macadam?"

She nodded. "Yes, Karyn—well, she shared with me that the artist lived right here in town and had a shop. I just wanted to meet you, to tell you how much I admire your work."

The woman beamed. "Well, call me Miss Trudy—and thank you, dear." She leaned forward and lowered her voice as if for privacy, which wasn't really necessary given they were the only ones currently in the shop. "Frankly, I do all these painting classes for the social aspect. I'm not one of those who can hole up for days on end with no people around, know what I mean? Anyway, the real profit is in my jewelry."

That made Lindsay's ears perk up. "Oh? Well, you are living my dream. My mother cautioned me away from a liberal arts degree, so I studied marketing in school, which is fascinating too in its own way. Still, while I love the business end of things, there remains something deep inside that longs to create."

Miss Trudy swept up next to her, folded her ample arm around her shoulders. "Oh, I know dear. Every artist is born with that same proclivity—to form things of beauty. I think it's a bit how we're like our Creator, I suppose."

Lindsay appreciated the understanding, and said so. "I'd love to see more of your work."

For the next several hours, the two of them huddled in Miss Trudy's back room, which was filled with windows overlooking a little garden area covered in snow. The inside walls were filled with brightly colored paintings and one wall was lined with shelves containing jars filled with beads, crystals and tiny spools of wire. Tools scattered a counter which ran the length of the wall.

"What a great place to work," Lindsay exclaimed.

"Oh, I know. This space is my personal haven." Miss Trudy waved her closer to a table filled with trays of stones and gems. Her new friend seemed delighted to share her knowledge.

"Gemstones are basically identified by their crystal structure, specific gravity, refractive index and other optical properties." She pointed to a certificate on the wall. "I highly recommend that if you are serious about this as a career, you get certified by the Gemological Association of America and that you join the American Gem Society. Both great organizations."

She paused, looked Lindsay directly in the eyes. "You know, that diamond on your hand is magnificent. Near perfect clarity."

Miss Trudy lifted a tray of gemstones in their rough state. "Ah—but I much prefer these treasures—filled with imperfections, but gorgeous just the same. These are some of my favorite pieces. All native to Idaho."

"All of those are local?"

Miss Trudy nodded. "Star garnets, citrine, amethyst and even some pink sapphires are found in the surrounding areas. But my favorites by far are fire opals. It's as if God's hand captured fire and light and encased them in translucent stone."

Several emotions chased across Lindsay's heart. It was as if she'd found a soul sister of sorts, someone else who was fascinated with taking nature's best, turning the precious items into objects of beauty.

"Can I ask you something rather personal?" she ventured.

"Sure, dear. Anything."

Lindsay straightened. "Can someone make a good living at this? I mean, do you think maybe I could?"

She was sure she saw a twinkle in the woman's eye. "I do very well. Could live anywhere I wanted, and my jewelry sales are at a level that allows me to live in one of the most upscale resort areas in America—in a nice home, I might add."

She grinned for good measure. "My sister and I travel all over the world when we want and I'm able to be generous with others in need. A very good life—and I'm grateful."

Sunlight poured into the room, and into her soul. Lindsay chewed at one of her nails as she contemplated what she was learning. Was it possible she could duplicate Miss Trudy's vocation? She had a lot to learn, but the thought thrilled her.

She stayed several more hours, absorbing everything Miss Trudy was willing to share.

Finally, she glanced at her watch. "Oh my goodness, I'm late! I was supposed to meet my fiancé for lunch. I've got to go." She quickly grabbed her purse.

Miss Trudy placed her plump fingers on Lindsay's sleeve, sending the bangles on her wrists jangling. "I've enjoyed this so much. It's not often I find someone who is as enthralled as I am with all of this." She swept her arms out wide. "Listen, why don't you stay over a few days. I'll help you. Show you how to design a collection and make it marketable. Share some of my secrets." Miss Trudy dangled the invitation out there, hopeful.

Lindsay allowed herself a moment to savor the possibility, considering what it might mean to have someone like Trudy Dilworth tutor her. The jumpstart to a potential career that would fire all her internal cylinders—both the creative and marketing sides of herself—well, it was simply too good to pass up. Besides, this could be the opportunity she most needed to clarify what she wanted her life to be going forward.

She couldn't help but give Miss Trudy a big hug. "I am going to do everything possible to work that out." She rushed for the door, waving. "And, Miss Trudy?"

"Yes, dear?"

"Thank you so much!"

CHAPTER THIRTEEN

Jess squeezed garlic cream cheese onto the last radicchio boat and stepped back to admire his work. He'd been up since dawn preparing for a large banquet for the Women in Film Institute.

Amelio DelCorte, the head chef, had been relying on him more and more in these past months. Sun Valley was enjoying a good snow year, business was up with the lodge at full capacity for the entire winter. That he'd been willing to step up and do double shifts when needed hadn't hurt either.

He untied his apron and hung it in his locker, alongside his white double-breasted jacket, then placed his toque blanche on the upper shelf. Many establishments had loose rules and the secondary chefs skipped the whole uniform thing, especially the hat. Amelio claimed that was a sign of sloppy neglect of their profession, and of the high standards held by the Sun Valley Resort.

Jess glanced at his watch. He had several hours before he'd have to be back for the banquet tonight. Perhaps he should go skiing with Brooke and the guys. Then again, something held him back.

A few minutes later, he found that *something* sitting alone at a table out by the ice skating rink. Her head was bent and she was writing in a notebook.

"Lindsay?" His heart pounded out of his chest. "Hey," he said, delighted to see her face break into a wide smile as she looked up at him. "Hope I'm not interrupting. You look pretty focused there." He pointed to the notebook.

Her grin turned sheepish. "You're not disturbing anything earth shattering. I was just dreaming . . . and sketching."

"Yeah?" He moved closer for a better look.

She pointed to a chair beside her, inviting him to join her. "I had the most marvelous morning," she gushed. "I met Trudy Dilworth. Did you know she was an accomplished jewelry artisan?"

"Miss Trudy? Sure. She makes great stuff."

Lindsay's eyes glistened with excitement. "I spent the last hours touring her studio, learning all about the craft and business. I had no idea Idaho had so many native gemstones."

She laughed at herself. "Sorry, I'm going on and on. What about you? I see a smile on your face. What's up?"

He wasn't about to tell her that finding her out here alone made him so happy. He didn't even want to admit the fact to himself. Truth was, he lost a lot of sleep last night thinking about her. About her soft hair and the way she smiled. About how she looked at him. The way they so easily connected. And—that she was engaged to be married. Which made her off limits.

He forced a light-hearted grin. "What's up with me? Well, I just stuffed two hundred snail shells with escargot and piped a filling in as many tiny lettuce leaves. I fired a sugar crust on trays of tiny ramekins filled with crème brulee custard and made sure the laundry service delivered plenty of fresh table linens for a big event tonight."

"Do you enjoy what you do?"

He nodded. "A lot. And I really like working here at the lodge. Great experience."

He studied her features, memorized the cute way the tip of her nose blushed ever so slightly when she was tickled over something, the faint spattering of freckles across her cheeks and the deep dimples on the side of her mouth.

Sure, he had extreme doubts that Tyler dude was the right one for her. He was a jerk! Still, that didn't give Jess the right to assess her choices and interfere with her future. He shouldn't even be out here with her now, because of the dangerous way he was feeling. But he couldn't help himself.

Besides, she was leaving tonight. That would be the end of it.

Until then, he'd indulge in these few minutes and enjoy being with her as friends, knowing he'd likely never see her again after this weekend.

An idea hit him. "Hey, do you skate?"

"Do I what?"

"Do you skate?"

She laughed. "I'm from the south. We don't

have a lot of ice skating rinks in Atlanta."

He stood and offered his hand. "Well then, c'mon. It's time you tried the ice."

She looked at him like he had two heads. "You can't be serious. Now?" She looked around as if she needed permission. "I mean, I don't think I would be able to—"

"Nonsense. Let's do it. You'll be able to go home to that fancy life of yours and be able to say you ice skated."

Her face clouded. "That's what you think? My life is fancy?"

Jess's gut turned in on itself. He could kick himself for being so flippant. "I didn't mean that how it sounded."

She slowly nodded. "Yes, you did. That's why I like you so much. You are one of the most authentic people I've ever met."

Did she just say she liked him? What did that mean exactly?

Feeling like a schoolboy, he took her hand and pulled her toward the ticket booth. He flashed his employee badge. "She's with me."

The young kid nodded. "You need skates?"

"Yeah." Jess turned to Lindsay. "What size?"

She told him and waited while Jess followed the kid into the back area. Moments later, he emerged with two pairs of skates. He sat and put his on first, then helped lace hers up before leading her onto the ice.

She wobbled and grabbed his shoulder laughing. "I feel like Bambi in that scene where Thumper and Flower are trying to be encouraging but Bambi's legs won't cooperate."

"Piece of cake. Just go slow. Start by holding your arms straight out at just below shoulder level to learn to balance by yourself. Like this." He showed her. "Try not to stiffen your body. It actually makes skating harder. Bend your knees slightly and lean forward."

She rested her hands on his shoulders and tried to follow his instructions.

"That's it. Exactly. You're doing it. You're ice skating!"

Lindsay beamed back at him. "I am! This southern belle is skating!"

She nearly toppled then, but he caught her. "Careful," he warned.

It wasn't long before she was able to glide across the ice, as long as he hung onto to her hand.

"Don't let go," she told him.

He paused, swallowed. "I won't." His promise was laced with words unspoken.

"I like seeing you so happy," he confessed, trying to sound lighthearted. "Like now—and when you were talking about Miss Trudy's studio."

She let his statement settle on her, grinned back at him. "Yes, I like being happy. Seems like I've felt nothing but stress since we got here, and certainly in the days leading up to this weekend. Honestly? I really don't want all this. I prefer simple, you know?"

He nodded. He knew exactly how she felt.

"I think that's what attracted me to the work that Miss Trudy does, how she takes something profoundly raw and basic from the earth and shapes it, polishes it into a thing of beauty that tells a story, sends a promise." She looked over at him. "Know what I mean?"

"You sound just like my grandmother. In fact, you remind me a lot of her. She passed when

I was twelve, but we were very close. She loved hunting agates in the Pioneer mountains and often took me with her. We found a great specimen of a rare pink agate on a hike on the Kane Lake Trailhead." He pointed to a mountain range to the northeast. "Wish we had time for me to take you up there. Show you around." He involuntarily tightened his grip on her hand.

She squeezed back, sadness spreading across her features. "I'm flying out tonight."

At that moment, her legs slipped out from under her and she landed in a heap on the ice, the motion taking him down with her. They stayed like that on the ice, unable to stop laughing.

"You okay?"

"Yeah. Just clumsy."

He shifted and as he did his palm slowly grazed the side of her arms as he tried to keep from crushing her small frame. "Sorry," he said, feeling her breath against his cheek. His pulse quickened. His mouth went dry.

She stopped laughing and looked in his eyes. She felt it too—this, whatever this was.

Before air could return to his lungs, his mouth moved to hers with gentle force. Her lips

165

were soft and tasted like marshmallow crème. A breathless moan escaped her lips as he kissed her. Softly at first, then with a deepened urgency.

She was so beautiful.

And she was taken.

The inner voice caused him to pull back with a start. "Lindsay, I—I'm so sorry. I never meant to—" His pulse thudded to a stop.

They both scrambled from the ice.

She looked as horrified as he felt. She glanced around, no doubt worried someone had seen them.

He reached for her. "Lindsay, I—"

She shook her head, held up open palms. "No—I can't."

She turned and quickly skated away, making her way to the edge of the rink. At the gate, she slid into a bench and scrambled to remove her skates.

He saw a flash of something on her face as she looked back at him that he'd never seen before—just a ghost of an expression, and in another state of mind he might not even have noticed it.

It was longing.

CHAPTER FOURTEEN

Lindsay's mom was busy packing when she returned to the room. "Well, there you are!" she said, not even bothering to look her way as she slid a sweater into her suitcase.

"How was breakfast?" Lindsay glossed over the comment and headed into the bathroom to check her reflection in the mirror, as if there might be some visible sign of what had transpired out on the skating rink, evidence of the conflict she felt that she needed to hide.

Having no intention of letting her off that easy, her mama poked her with a bit of interrogation. "Where'd you take off to this morning? You were sleeping so soundly this morning, I thought I wouldn't wake you. But I left a note, thought you might join us for breakfast."

Lindsay knew her mother had not extended a warm invitation in that note. Just the contrary—her mother was ticked at her, and still was. But in the ways of southern women, she was far too polite to admit it outright. Her mother had learned the art of sidestepping any uncomfortable situation, while still getting her point across.

"We had the best eggs benedict," she went on. "The hollandaise was rich and lemony and the eggs poached to a perfect firmness. I hate when the yolks run all over the plate."

Lindsay knew her mother would also cringe if she knew how her daughter's emotions were now running all over the place.

There was no denying her attraction to Jess Barnett. How fun and spontaneous, and amazingly authentic he was. Or, how she felt when he'd kissed her.

Yes—she'd only known him for a few days. None of this made sense.

Neither did the quiet doubt in her choice to marry Tyler DeLuca—the growing insistence that she was making a big mistake.

She'd thought she loved him—she did. But was love enough?

There was no arguing their hopes and dreams did not intersect—that they were two people who perhaps weren't meant to be together.

Even so, once fuel boosters are lit and the launch sequence begins sending the rocket barreling into space, it's no easy task to turn the speeding missile back to the launch pad—even if you want to.

"Honey, did you hear what I said?"

"Huh? Oh, sorry. What did you need, Mama?"

"I asked what you and Tyler's plans were for this afternoon."

"I haven't checked with him," Lindsay admitted. Then to cover up, she added, "He had a busy morning. I thought it might be best not to bother him. He'll call when he's free."

That seemed to satisfy her mother. She nodded. "Well, I'm going to run over to that little boutique in the village and pick up some souvenirs. Give you time to pack."

Lindsay sighed with relief when the door

closed behind her. Yes, she needed some time alone—she had a lot of baggage to deal with.

And she wasn't talking about her suitcases.

* * *

Even though the room was plenty warm, Jess jabbed at the fire embers with the poker like he was killing a Copperhead in Texas. He took off his cap, wiped his brow with his sleeve. "Anybody bother to clean this fireplace flue in the last six months?" Without waiting for a response, he tossed the poker onto the hearth.

Abe got up from the sofa. "Hey, what's with you?"

Lacking the grace to look sheepish, Jess ignored his buddy's sarcastic tone. "I'm just making a point that—"

"The point that ever since you got home you've been in a mood?" Abe grabbed his empty glass from the coffee table and headed for the kitchen.

Brooke took the glass from Abe's hand and moved for the sink. She squirted some dish soap and turned on the faucet. "I thought you would be doing cartwheels and making snow angels after getting that text from Karyn Macadam."

"What text?" Abe asked.

She turned off the faucet and grabbed the dish rag, turned and nodded in Jess's direction. "Meet the new sous chef at the Sun Valley Lodge."

"What? Hey man, that's great!" Abe shook his head, confused. "But then why the bad mood?"

Jess huffed. "I'm not in a bad mood. I just have a lot on my mind."

Brooke returned to the task of washing Abe's glass. "That would mean staying in Sun Valley permanently. That's a good thing, right?"

Jess didn't answer as he grabbed for his guitar. He sunk to the sofa and strummed a few chords.

He didn't have to look up to know that Abe and Brooke were exchanging glances.

"Hey," Abe said. "This is about that chick isn't it?"

Jess took a deep breath. "Maybe," he admitted. "Doesn't matter. First, Lindsay Griffin is way out of my league. And unless you two grinning fools forgot, she's very much engaged."

The truth stabbed him in the heart. He rarely dated, and now he'd let himself fall for someone he could never have? Real smart.

"I know what you're thinking. Dude . . . she's hot. And anyone within twelve feet can see she's not that into the rich guy as much as she thought."

"I agree, Jess." Brooke put the glass in the drainer, folded the rag and placed it on the counter next to the sink. "She's not going to be happy with Tyler DeLuca. You have to do something—and quick."

He agreed. Lindsay was hot. And nice. And smart. He'd give anything to change the way things were. Just because Tyler was the wrong one didn't necessarily mean he was the right one—or that she felt the same way he did.

"I need to stay out of the way, let her come to her own conclusions—make a decision for herself without me muddying everything up for her."

Jess tossed his cap on the table, ran his hand through hair before leaning his guitar against the sofa. He thought about what had happened out on the ice—the way he'd allowed his emotions to override his good sense.

Brooke walked over, placed her hand on his shoulder. "Jess, listen to us. You can't let her leave without telling her exactly how you feel. Yes, the decision is hers—but don't rob her of knowing what choices are before her."

His gaze dropped to the floor. "I kissed her. Today at the ice rink." He swallowed and confessed to his friends what had happened, how she'd looked at him. "Doesn't matter. In the end, she's still leaving with the other guy. I think it's best to leave good enough alone."

Abe rolled his eyes. "Dude, she wasn't with her fiancé the morning after her engagement party. She was hanging out with you. What does that tell you?" His friend paused, allowing his words to sink in. "Now go get her."

Jess considered Abe's comment for several seconds, let the impact make its way into his thinking.

He stood and grabbed his coat. "I'll be back later!"

Brooke beamed. "You going to go see Lindsay? Tell her how you feel?"

"No," he said, heading for the door. "I'm heading over to see Miss Trudy."

CHAPTER FIFTEEN

Lindsay was unusually somber as she stood on the balcony. Never had she felt so conflicted.

She'd kissed another man.

Even if she and Jess hadn't planned to cross the line, there was no missing how his kiss had rattled her heart. When their lips met, everything shifted.

At that moment, she realized her relationship with Tyler no longer simply teetered on a fault line. The foundation beneath them had indeed completely crumbled.

She rubbed her arms against the chill and wandered back inside.

She was so stupid. How had she allowed this to happen? No matter which direction she turned, there would be irreparable consequences.

Emotions weren't buttons you could simply push on and off. A part of her loved Tyler. A future with him would be secure, predictable. Yet, she undoubtedly would grow to regret their incompatibility, the loss of her own hopes and dreams.

Even more, there was no missing what had passed between she and Jess out on the ice. A guy she'd known less than a weekend had looked straight at her, into her, anchoring her.

Every time she was with him, she felt as transparent as Saran Wrap and just as fragile. There was no hiding from his gaze. He seemed to acutely sense her deep need for authentic connection, and longed for nothing more than to fill her empty places—to make her smile.

Lindsay touched her lips, remembering the way they tingled after the kiss.

Did she have feelings for Jess? Feelings that went beyond friendship?

Before she could chase that thought, there was a noise outside the door. Mama must be having trouble with her entry card. She sighed. "Hold on, Mama. I'm coming," she called out.

She swung the door open. Her breath caught in her throat.

Jess stood on the other side.

* * *

The moment the door opened, Jess wished he'd had the good sense to listen to his own instincts and not follow his friends' advice. What was he thinking just showing up like this? It was stupid, and he'd live to regret making a fool of himself.

Lindsay looked shocked to see him. "Jess?" She quickly glanced up and down the hall. "What are you doing here?"

His heart pounded with a case of sudden nerves. This had sounded like such a good idea an hour ago. Now he wasn't so sure. "I—I wanted to say goodbye. I mean, I didn't want that last—" He paused. "Is your mother here?"

A tiny smile sprouted at the corners of her lips. "No. I'm alone."

Relieved, he went on. "I didn't want what happened out at the ice skating rink to be our goodbye. You're my friend. I crossed the line out there. That's not how I want you to remember me."

"It wasn't only you. I mean—"

Their eyes met. "I know what you mean," he said, nodding.

Lindsay stepped back and waved him inside. "Would you like to come in?"

He shook his head. "I don't think that's a very good idea. I just wanted to give you something."

"Me?"

"Yeah." He dug in his pocket and pulled out a clumsily wrapped box. "Here." He steadied his trembling fingers and handed over the gift. "Don't open it now," he cautioned. "Wait until later, when you're alone, okay?"

She smiled. That drop dead gorgeous smile that had ensnared him in the first place. A pleasant warmth spread through him as he stared, memorizing every feature so he could carry her with him after she was gone.

With Tyler.

He swallowed. "Well, that's all. I mean, I'd

better go." He turned and took a tentative step toward the elevator.

Jess looked back, saw her standing in the doorway watching. "Hey, I forgot to tell you," he said with a bit of excitement. "I got a new job. You're looking at the new sous chef here at Sun Valley Lodge."

Her face broke into genuine pleasure at the news. "Oh, Jess. That's wonderful. I'm so happy for you."

"Yeah, means I stay put for a while." He swallowed again, hard. "I wish you much happiness too, Lindsay. You deserve it."

Before he wavered and ran back to her, begged her to reconsider her engagement and stay with him to find out where all this might lead, he forced himself to take a final look.

"Take care," he said, then he quickly moved into the elevator and punched the button for the lobby.

* * *

Lindsay stared at the closed elevator doors for

179

several seconds before she turned and went back inside her room. Slowly, she shut the door while holding tightly to the tiny box.

She glanced at the bedside clock. Her mama would be returning at any time.

Unable to stifle her curiosity, she sunk to an overstuffed chair by the fireplace and fingered the box.

Sadness built in her gut as she contemplated his goodbye, the look in his eyes as those elevator doors closed. There was no denying how Jess Barnett felt about her, and if she were completely honest she had to admit she had feelings for him as well, which made for a bit of a crazy circus going on in her head.

She'd arrived in Sun Valley only days ago on a high knowing full well what the future held. Now, all her perfect plans had plummeted into a pool of doubt and confusion. She didn't know how she felt about anything anymore. Not really.

Irritation nestled, moved inside as she fought hard against the intruding idea that she was about to marry a man who didn't grasp the things she cared about the most—her fiancé just didn't get it.

Wait—was that even true? How could he spend the amount of time with her that he had, love her and want to make her his wife if he didn't get it?

Because he never listens to you—that's why.

The truth hit yet again, causing an emotional subterranean shift. He'd hurt her, even if he hadn't meant to. Though he'd never admit it, he'd been attracted to the very qualities he now seemed to despise in her.

Worse, he was a minion under his father's control, and attitudes. He'd not likely free himself of those chains unless he left the family business, which was never going to happen.

And there was still the lingering issue of his lack of respect.

A dizzying sense of inevitability enveloped her as she untied the pretty lavender ribbon and let it fall away from the patterned gift wrap. Carefully, she lifted the tape from the wrapped end of the box, noting the way the ends failed to meet perfectly—a fact that made her smile.

She drew a breath, slipped the paper aside. Her fingers trembled ever so slightly as she lifted the lid on the box.

Inside, on a simple bed of cotton, was a hypnotically beautiful pendant, a snake chain with organically shaped sterling wrapped around a highly polished pink cabochon.

Her voice wobbled as she spoke out loud. "His grandmother's pink agate."

What Jess had done hit her. He'd taken something of extreme personal value and had gifted it to her. A lump rose in her throat as she considered his gesture.

With reverent care, she lifted the pendant and fingered the top of the rare stone, appreciating the way tiny filaments of rose threaded through plumes of cotton candy pink in a beautiful pattern that reminded her of light shining through clouds.

Only days before, she looked out the bathroom window and saw Jess for the first time. She remembered the way they'd traded smiles and the odd pull he'd had on her, how the encounter left her feeling a little off balance. When they'd run into each other again in the hallway, she couldn't help but notice the way his t-shirt clung to his broad chest and strong shoulders, but even more the way his brown eyes seemed to look right into her soul.

A familiar rush of adrenaline left her unsettled as she thought about the way the damp curls of his hair carelessly brushed his neck as he'd effortlessly glided through the snow, his cheeks red with the chill of the air.

Lindsay drew a deep breath.

Her lips curved into a smile as her mind returned to the moment out on the ice when in a flash they'd gone down laughing, how the heat of his body warmed her own. The pads of his fingers brushed against the fabric covering her arm, she heard the sharp intake of breath as he gazed into her eyes. Seconds later his lips touched hers. He took her mouth, stole her breath. His lips moved with sureness, possessing her.

One thing she knew, Jess Barnett never pushed her to the sideline. He made her feel cherished.

Lindsay bit the tender flesh inside her mouth. Moisture welled onto her lashes as she imagined what life might be—with Jess.

Perhaps they would live in a tiny house with a

yard bordering the Wood River. She could see him grilling steaks, hear the laughter of their children as they chased through the shade of quaking aspen trees. She would work to make pendants as beautiful as the one in the box in her hands, to sell in her own shop. Jess would be her biggest fan.

Her daddy often quoted Abraham Lincoln. "The best way to predict your future is to create it."

The steps she took now would dictate the fate of her own happiness. Choices were hard, but necessary.

She could not live for Tyler, or her mother. She had a destiny all her own, one worth stepping into.

In a sudden moment of clarity, she knew what she had to do.

Lindsay swallowed and lifted her wrist, unhooked the delicate clasp on the diamond bracelet and slipped it from her wrist. Next, she wiggled the expensive engagement ring from her finger.

Outside the windows, snow fell gently from the sky as she slipped both in her jeans pocket and headed for the door.

CHAPTER SIXTEEN

Lindsay had wanted to meet with Tyler somewhere quiet, where they could talk without interruption. Tyler insisted he was in the mood for a grilled steak and suggested they take the opportunity to check out Crusty's before it was time to head for the airport, a little bar run by a proprietor who had a reputation for serving up some of the best food in town, mainly to the locals.

Nerves caused a trail of moisture to trickle down Lindsay's neck as Tyler guided her through the congested bar to a table near the pool table. She found herself wishing she hadn't worn a ski sweater. The outside frigid air had masked the heat she'd experience inside.

Once seated, she glanced around. The men

sitting at the bar looked to be friends given the way they were chatting. To her right, a cute girl with long brown hair was playing pool with a guy who had a bear tattoo on his forearm.

Tyler pulled a plastic menu from a rack next to the salt and pepper shakers on their table. "You hungry? I'm starved."

She'd lost her appetite hours ago. Even so, she grabbed a menu and scanned the selections, settling on something simple. "I'll just have a hamburger."

A waitress with too-red lipstick took their order. Then they were alone.

Lindsay knew she must say what she had to say—and fast. She glanced to their right, then left, making sure they would not be overheard. She swallowed. "Tyler, I need to talk to you."

The waitress suddenly reappeared and plucked down two frosty mugs of beer. She gave Lindsay a weak smile before retreating.

"What is it, Babe?" Tyler took a long draw from his beer and set his mug down. "If it's about this morning, look I couldn't do anything about—"

She held up a palm and shook her head. "It's not about this morning."

Tyler looked momentarily relieved. He leaned back, checked out the sports scores on the television mounted on the opposite wall.

With trembling fingers, she reached in her pocket, lifted out the ring and bracelet and slid them across the table, amazed he hadn't noticed her vacant ring finger earlier.

He reached for his beer, noticed the items on the table and scowled. "What's this?" He leaned in, took a closer look. Puzzled, he lifted his gaze to her. "Lindsay?"

Her heart thudded slowly. "Tyler, I'm sorry." She pinned him with a look and her throat turned dry as desert sand. "I can't marry you."

He studied her, his head cocked to the side. After a moment of awkwardness, he finally spoke. "Clearly, we have a lot to discuss." His tone held a challenge, but she wouldn't buy in. She needed for him to understand.

"I'm not flying back with you. I'm going to stay in Sun Valley. There's a woman named Trudy Dilworth and—"

"I know Trudy."

"Well—Miss Trudy has agreed to mentor me."

He scoffed. "Mentor you? In what?"

She straightened her shoulders, resolved. "In jewelry making. I've done a lot of thinking." She reached and touched his forearm. "I can't live the life being your wife would require, Tyler. That lifestyle is just not me. I want something very different."

Lindsay knew she'd punched him in the gut.

Darkness thundered across his brow and his jaw went slack. "Is this about that guy—that ski bum?"

"We're friends." The words felt soiled coming out. She didn't want to make this worse by admitting the relationship might turn into something more. Besides, she didn't need to.

Lindsay's breath caught in her lungs as Tyler held her captive with his pointed look. He knew. He knew she cared for Jess. Thought she was a fool for changing her mind.

Sometimes, changing course was the courageous thing to do. She knew that now.

Tyler met her gaze, his eyes flinching for just a second. She watched the emotions dancing across his face. He'd never been good at hiding his feelings.

Lindsay let silence further establish the space between them, let the sound of a pool cue hitting balls into table pockets fill the gap.

Tyler's expression changed, grew serious. His tone was cool and collected. "I don't suppose there's anything I can say that will change your mind? You're making a huge mistake, Lindsay. Think about your future, and mine. I mean—" He let his words drift as the reality of what was happening sunk in.

"Look, Tyler—I know saying I'm sorry doesn't erase the pain and humiliation," she choked out. Was it foolish to dream that someday Tyler would be able to remember her with fondness, and not hatred?

She swallowed. "I hope you can forgive me."

The pause that followed was so long, Lindsay thought Tyler wasn't going to answer. When he finally did, she was relieved. He smiled and she saw a glimpse of the old Tyler. "Well, at least you won't have to deal with our mothers," he said, pushing past the rejection he had to be wrestling.

Silence fell again as he slipped the jewelry pieces from the table and slipped them in his pocket. "Do you want to tell me why?"

She tempered her next words with grace, remembering all the good times they'd shared. "Tyler, a part of me will always love you. But, I'm not meant to be the wife you need me to be. You're not the husband I need. In some ways, I think we've both known that at some level but we just kept moving forward anyway."

The waitress appeared juggling heavy plates filled with their food. Sadly, Lindsay was no longer hungry. Neither was Tyler.

"Look," he said. "You stay on at the lodge for a few days until you get settled and have things all figured out. My credit card will cover anything you need." He pushed the plate aside and stood. "I'll have my secretary rebook your flight."

In an unexpected and poignant move, Tyler lifted her chin so she would have to face him. "So, I guess this is goodbye." He leaned then and kissed her lightly on the forehead. "Take care,

Lindsay."

He shifted away a few steps, tossed some bills onto the bar and walked away.

Even though she knew she'd made the right decision, it felt as though someone were sitting on her chest as she watched him go.

She sat alone, her hand over the space between her breast and stomach, willing her heartbeat to return to the reliable rhythm she once knew. Finally, she exhaled a shaky breath, stood and headed for the door herself.

Minutes later, bright, crisp winter air washed across her face as she stepped outside and into her new life.

CHAPTER SEVENTEEN

It was harder to tell her mother, but Lindsay simply explained the decision to call off the wedding was hers, and hers alone.

"Mom, I found what will make me happy and it's not living in an affluent townhouse nestled up against Central Park as Mrs. Tyler DeLuca. I'm sorry."

"Is it that Jess person? He's the one who changed your mind."

"Partly," she admitted. "But not as entirely as you might think. This is where I belong."

Her mother huffed. "Lindsay Kaye, we're from the south. Not the Idaho mountains."

She arched her brow. "But I belong in New York?"

Her mother tapped her sandaled foot, her glittery pink toenails rising and falling. "You're making a huge mistake. I wish you'd listen to reason."

Lindsay closed her eyes and took a deep breath. When she opened her eyes again, she looked at her mother, determined to respond with patience. "Daddy would approve. He lived with no regrets." She reached and took her mother's hand and brought it to her lips. "I love you, Mama. So very much. But I'm not living your life—I'm living mine."

* * *

Lindsay stood in the lobby. She waved at Karyn at the concierge desk. "Hey, Karyn—have you seen Jess? I think he's supposed to be working this afternoon."

Karyn grinned and pointed down a hallway. "Follow me. I'll take you to the kitchen."

Jess was standing with his back to them, peeling potatoes into a stainless steel sink. Finished, he tossed the peeler onto the counter and turned, wiped his hands on his apron. "Hey," he said, clearly surprised. "What are you doing here?"

"This VIP guest wanted to see you," Karyn said, smiling. "And we always try to make our guests happy." She winked over at Lindsay before retreating, leaving the two of them alone.

Lindsay moved deliberately forward, stopping a few paces in front of Jess. She lifted her hand and showed him the space where her engagement ring had been, and was no longer.

Jess looked at her, confused. "What? I—I don't understand."

She grinned and fingered the pendant hanging from her neck. "I guess I found a new stone . . . one that better suits me."

"Are you serious?" He dropped his apron to the floor and lifted her, swung her wildly in a circle. "That's friggin' crazy!" He set her down, ran a hand through his hair. "And wonderful!"

Lindsay laughed, joy bubbling inside for the first time in a long while. Then she did something neither one of them expected.

She kissed him.

Enjoy the first chapter from

Sisters

Book One of the Sun Valley Series

CHAPTER ONE

Karyn Macadam slowed her car as the sign to the Hemingway Memorial came into view. She turned off Sun Valley Road into the parking area, not bothering to signal. There was no need, not at this early hour.

Cutting the engine, she sat quietly for a few moments, the radio blaring in the background.

And we expect another warm summer day here in the Wood River Valley as residents in this popular resort area prepare to commemorate one of its own, nearly a year and a half after the tragic accident that took the life of—

Karyn shut off the radio, her heart thudding painfully.

Squeezing the steering wheel, she refused to look at the seat next to her—at the small wooden box intricately carved with falling snowflakes over a set of crossed skis.

Deep breath in. Deep breath out.

Five more minutes she sat there, putting off what was ahead.

Finally, she scooped the box into her hands and climbed out of the car.

She'd made a promise. One she fully intended to keep, even if she'd made it a bit tongue-in-cheek at the time.

Gravel crunched beneath her feet as she traversed the walkway toward the memorial. Even in the faint morning light she could make out wild poppies and blue flax, delicate against the pungent skunk cabbage jutting from the pebbled ground lining the trail.

The sound of water bubbling across a rocky streambed pulled her toward the monument nested against a stand of aspen trees, their tiny dollar-shaped leaves barely moving in the still air.

It was understandable why the famous novelist had loved Idaho, why he'd spent his last days living here. Ernest Hemingway was only one of many celebrities who had traded big city tangled traffic for cool mountain mornings and alpine vistas and made Sun Valley their residence.

Olympic hopeful Dean Macadam was another.

Karyn stood at the water's edge and looked past the pile of flat stones with its stately column rising from the middle, beyond the trees to the golf course in the distance. A deer standing in the middle of one of the greens lifted its head and stared back at her in mutual regard.

A voice in her head rang out as clear as if Dean were standing next to her.

"What is your fascination with Hemingway anyway?"

She closed her eyes, remembered gazing up from the pages of *For Whom the Bell Tolls*. "Are you crazy? He was only the best American novelist of all time," she'd so flippantly reminded her husband.

Dean playfully tugged at the sheet tucked around her bare waist. "Is that so?"

She quickly snatched the covering from his hands and secured it more tightly. "Yes, that's so. In fact, Ernest Hemingway is known for his mastery of theme and imagery. Take this story for example." She held up the heavy volume borrowed from her dad, its cover worn from repeated readings. "The entire narrative is punctuated with a preoccupation with death and dying, which is so poignant given his eventual suicide."

Dean ran broad fingers through his sleep-tousled hair. "Yeah, you see—that's what I don't get. Why is so many people's imagination captured with a guy who spent an inordinate amount of time writing about life instead of living it? I mean, in my view, that's likely what led to him offing himself in the end."

She raised her gaze in horror and slammed the book against her new husband's chest. "Don't say that."

He laughed. "Okay, okay—look, I get it.

Ernest Hemingway is your book boyfriend. I'm not jealous. Really I'm not." His eyes nearly sparkled when he'd said that. "Tell you what. When I die, you just take my ashes and toss them in that little creek that runs in front of his memorial. That way, when I'm gone, you can visit both of us at the same time."

Before she could protest the macabre suggestion, he pulled the novel from her and tossed it to the floor, while at the same time lifting the sheet with his other hand.

She'd giggled as he buried his head against her skin. "Promise me. Even if my mother protests and wants otherwise," he said, in a muffled voice. "Now. Promise. Or, I'll—" His fingers dug into her sides and he tickled, sending her entire torso into a fit of squirming. "Promise," he repeated.

"I promise. I promise," she shouted, laughing uncontrollably.

He immediately stopped tickling. "Okay, that's better." Her new husband looked at her then, his eyes boring into her soul. "And promise you'll always remember I love you."

The sound of his voice still seemed so real, even after all these months. She sunk to the curved stone bench. Tears collected in her eyes and spilled over, making their way down her cheeks. She fingered the familiar lid on the box.

I'm sorry, Dean. I can't do it.

No matter that she'd gotten out of her bed while it was still dark outside with the best intentions. She still wasn't ready to let him go.

Not now—and maybe never.

* * *

Grayson Chandler wrangled his way past a bunch of willow branches, taking care not to break his fly rod, then headed south crossing into a clearing.

That's when he saw her.

Early thirties. Coffee-colored long hair. Sitting quietly on the stone bench at the Hemingway Memorial.

Not really understanding why, he quieted his steps as he approached.

She held something in her hands, a little box. Her head was tucked. Was she—?

Holding his breath, he moved closer.

Yes, she was crying.

He crouched behind a clump of thick brush and watched, knowing he was encroaching, but unable to help himself.

She was a pretty gal. Frankly, she reminded him a whole lot of that royal lady in England. What was her name? Not Princess Diana, but her son's wife.

Unable to remember, he shook his head. Didn't matter.

What mattered was that she was openly weeping now.

He wavered. Should he step forward? Offer her assistance? He shook his head. Naw— probably not. It wasn't like he carried a handkerchief in his pocket like his dad used to. Likely she just needed some time to get whatever was bothering her out of her system. Women were like that.

Still, he couldn't help but think whatever she was spilling about was not the least bit inconsequential. Clearly, she was torn up.

Ignoring the reprimanding voice inside that

warned him he was being voyeuristic, he rested his fly pole on the ground and continued to watch.

Even crying, she was beautiful, what with her thick lashes sweeping across ivory cheeks that looked as soft as a rose petal. He knotted his hand and pressed it against his lips, imagining brushing his thumb across her skin.

He hadn't thought about a woman in that way for a really long time. Not since—well, since Robin. A subject he didn't care to think about.

The woman on the bench wiped her face with the back of her hand and looked up toward the sky. A few seconds later, she fingered the top of the little wooden box in her lap, chewing at her lip.

Finally, she stood and gazed into the trees, tears still rimming her lashes.

He battled a surge of protectiveness, yet remained still. Under different circumstances he might take a chance, go introduce himself. But he knew better this time.

She turned and saw him. Frowning, she pulled the little box close to her chest.

Face flushed, he reached for his pole and

stood. "Hey, I'm sorry. I didn't mean to—what I meant is, I just didn't want to interrupt—" He shook his head. "Look, I'm sorry."

Judging from the way she fidgeted, she too was embarrassed. She tucked a strand of hair behind her ear. "I—I thought I was alone."

"I wasn't really watching. I was doing a little fly fishing." He pointed back at the creek. "I saw you and—"

She rubbed at the place between her eyebrows, then dropped her hand. "Look, I really need to go." She turned and starting walking toward the parking lot.

He wanted to say something more, maybe get her name, but thought better of it.

Upon reaching her car, she glanced back.

In an awkward attempt to apologize again for his intrusion on her private moments, he nodded and gave her a faint smile.

Inside, he wanted to kick himself.

Afterword

Hey, everybody—Karyn Macadam here, fictional hospitality director for the Sun Valley Lodge. Kellie and I are so glad you joined us for the debut story in the **LOVE ON VACATION** books. These shorter length romances invite readers to come on vacation with characters who travel to Sun Valley and stay at the iconic Sun Valley Lodge. This groundbreaking series is packed with tales of dating and mating, love and marriage and promises to keep your emotions and funny bone on high alert.

I hope you enjoyed following Jess and Lindsay's journey to their happily ever after! I know I did. (I knew from minute one that Tyler just wasn't the right guy for Lindsay—didn't you?)

Friends, Kellie is writing as fast as she can to bring us even more stories.

Make sure and sign up for her **newsletter** at www.kelliecoatesgilbert.com/contact/#sign-up so you get notices when future books in the series are available. Don't forget to check out all the information on Sun Valley she has on her **website** at www.kelliecoatesgilbert.com   (PS—that's   her hometown area!)

You might also enjoy Kellie's new romantic women's fiction stories—the **_SUN VALLEY SE-RIES_** www.kelliecoatesgilbert.com/books. These stories feature my family and are set in America's first destination ski resort, starting with **_SISTERS_** www.kelliecoatesgilbert.com/books, which offers a thought-provoking look at me and my sisters and the choices we make when we realize our lives aren't exactly what we expected. One thing I've learned—through romance and heartbreak, laughter and tears . . . life is always better with your sisters by your side.

I hope you'll come alongside and follow our stories! See you soon!

~Karyn

About the Author

Kellie Coates Gilbert has won readers' hearts with her compelling and highly emotional stories about women and the relationships that define their lives. A former legal investigator, she is especially known for keeping readers turning pages and creating nuanced characters who seem real.

In addition to garnering hundreds of starred reader reviews, Kellie has been described by RT Book Reviews as a "deft, crisp storyteller." Her books were featured as Barnes & Noble Top Shelf Picks and were included on Library Journal's Best Book List of 2014.

Born and raised near Sun Valley, Idaho, Kellie now lives with her husband of over thirty-five years in Dallas, where she spends most days by her pool drinking sweet tea and writing the stories of her heart.

Please visit her at:
www.kelliecoatesgilbert.com

Don't miss out on new releases and special contest information! If you haven't signed up for **Kellie's newsletter** . . . what are you waiting for?
www.kelliecoatesgilbert.com/contact/#sign-up

Also by Kellie Coates Gilbert:

Mother of Pearl
A Woman of Fortune
Where Rivers Part
A Reason to Stay
What Matters Most
Sisters (Sun Valley Series Book 1)
Otherwise Engaged – a Love on Vacation Story

More information and purchase links can be
found at: www.kelliecoatesgilbert.com

Made in the USA
Coppell, TX
10 December 2019